HER MISTLETOE COWBOY

A BUTTARS BROTHERS NOVEL, STEEPLE RIDGE ROMANCE BOOK 4

LIZ ISAACSON

"Therefore the Lord himself shall give you a sign; behold, a virgin shall conceive, and bear a son, and shall call his name Immanuel."

~Isaiah 7:14

CHAPTER
ONE

"Logan, Ben needs you."

Logan smiled at the woman who'd come to get him. He thought it was one of Rae's friends, someone from the rec center. She had hair halfway between blonde and red, and she practically wilted under Logan's smile.

He wiped it away as soon as he went past her. He wouldn't be getting a date while at his brother's wedding. Oh no. Today was all about Ben and Rae—and everyone else in Island Park, as it seemed the whole blasted town had shown up for the nuptials.

"Ben?" He pushed into the shed in the corner of the huge Sports Complex where Rae had insisted they get married.

"Over here. I can't tie this stupid thing." Ben sounded frustrated and nervous at the same time. Logan didn't blame him. When their oldest brother's plane had been delayed by two hours because of a freak hailstorm in Wyoming, both Ben and Logan had grown concerned.

Logan crossed the concrete to Ben. "He's going to get here." Sam was supposed to be the one helping Ben get dressed. Making sure every button was done up right, and the bow tie got proper square tips.

"Have you heard from him?"

"Yeah, they touched down an hour ago."

"The wedding is in thirty minutes."

"Well, probably sixty." Logan grinned at Ben, who stared at him with a hint of danger in his eyes. "Relax, Ben. Everyone's fine. You should see them sucking down that punch Rae won't give us the recipe for."

That got Ben to smile. "It's just almond flavoring."

"If that were true." Logan focused on the bow tie and got it looking decent. "She'd tell us the recipe."

"I'll get it out of her eventually."

Logan chuckled. "Right. Because married couples don't have secrets."

"I swear, we don't," Ben said. "It's just the punch, which she claims isn't really her recipe to give out. It's her mother's."

"And you're not married yet," Logan said. "So it's okay if Rae has secrets still."

"She doesn't have secrets," Ben insisted, which only made Logan smile wider. He loved teasing his brothers, especially Ben.

Logan stepped back and scanned his brother. "Looks good, bro. Nice and pressed."

Ben tugged at the sleeves of his jacket. "It's hot."

"You're the one who chose the first weekend of September to get married."

"That was Rae. She said the park would be amazing in the fall."

Logan shook his head and clucked his tongue. "Blaming her already."

Ben gave Logan a playful shove. "Go on. Get out of here. Go make sure we don't run out of punch." He tacked on a laugh, and Logan went because Darren came in. "He's nervous," Logan whispered to his twin as he passed.

Darren simply nodded. The more serious of the two, Darren had stepped up to take care of everything since Sam had gotten married and left town a couple of months ago. An intense wave of missing hit Logan right in the chest, where he struggled to breathe against it. But breathe he did, because he spotted Rae's mother and he was determined to get that punch recipe before the ceremony began.

"This is the best punch I've ever tasted," he said in a booming voice that echoed under the tents that had been set up. "Rae tells me it's your recipe."

Beth Cantwell smiled at him. "It sure is."

"So we're almost family now." Logan downed a mouthful of punch, the craving to do so again immediate and intense. There was definitely more in this punch than simply almond flavoring. The carbonation pinged against his throat as he swallowed.

"That we are." Beth continued talking, but her words fell into Logan's deaf ears. He blinked, and where there had once been a sea of people, now there only existed Layla Guyman.

She wore a floor-length gown the color of midnight, and Logan's mouth turned as dry as the Sahara. This wasn't the first time he'd had this reaction to the curvy blonde veterinarian. Oh no. He'd nearly rammed into the doorway at the church the first time he'd seen her. The second had almost left him with a broken toe as he'd lifted his foot to step onto the curb and didn't quite get his leg high enough.

She'd seemed interested in him too, but she'd pulled back, back, back, until Logan figured she wasn't. He'd put his feelings in a box on a shelf in the back of his mind, but they'd burst free at the sight of her so-blonde-it-was-almost-white hair swept off her neck and into a wedding up-do to out-do all other up-do's. Her skin had been kissed by the summer sun, and Logan wanted to touch her arm, hold her hand, skate his fingers along her jaw before he kissed her. Even from across the distance, he found the joy and sparkle in her intense blue eyes, and he suddenly wanted her gaze on his.

"Who are you starin' at?"

Logan clamped his mouth shut and startled, nearly spilling his almond concoction down the front of his suit. "No one." He glanced at Tucker, who'd appeared out of nowhere. Tucker, who now scanned the crowd where Logan had indeed been staring.

"Where's Missy?" Logan asked, hoping to distract his boss.

"You know, you should've excused yourself before drifting off into a stare-fest," Tucker said, completely undeterred.

"What are you talking about?"

"You were talking to Rae's mother. Now she thinks you might have special needs, because you just, and I quote, 'sort of went mute' and she 'couldn't get your attention'." Tucker sipped from his own glass of punch. "So who was it? Rita?"

Logan pressed his lips together. Rita had brown hair. Not bad brown hair, but Logan much preferred blondes.

"Not Rita. Okay." Tucker took longer to look at the crowd mingling under the tents. Logan had never wanted Sam to show up as badly as he did right now. But Sam was probably still at least forty-five minutes away, and there weren't all that many women for Tucker to choose from.

Thankfully, Tucker had only named four women before his wife joined them. "Tucker, have you heard from Sam?"

"No." He looked at Logan. "You?"

"He texted when they landed. He should be here in about thirty minutes." Logan started to edge away from Tucker and Missy, but the glint in Tucker's eyes meant he hadn't forgotten about Logan's "special needs" behavior.

He found Rae's mother and said, "I'm so sorry, Miss Beth. I saw someone I hadn't in a while, and I sort of zoned out."

She accepted his apology with grace but made a hasty escape with a silver-haired man Logan had never seen before. He sighed as he turned, planning to get more punch and find the coolest patch of shade he could.

He ran right into Layla instead. "Oof," he grunted at the same time she exclaimed, "Oh!"

He reached out and put his hand on her shoulder to

steady her, one of his fantasies roaring to life. Her skin against his fingers felt like silk and magic, and Logan lost his voice completely.

This is Layla, he told himself. They'd been friends for two years, even though she'd gone through a cold spell with him. He volunteered at the veterinary clinic where Layla worked twice a week. He saw her all the time at church functions, at work, around town.

But he'd never seen her like this.

"Nothing spilled." She scanned herself and then lifted her eyes to his, her glorious smile lighting up the entire park. "So we're good."

"Good," Logan echoed stupidly, wondering why his feelings for Layla had to be so present today of all days. He cleared his throat and tried to center his thoughts. He'd dated before. Women didn't scare him.

Layla sure did though. He managed to ask, "Have you tried that almond punch?"

"I've had it loads of times," she said. "I still can't get Rae to give me the recipe." Her eyes were so blue, Logan thought they had to be fake. Her hair color certainly was, though Logan hadn't seen a dark root in all the time he'd known her. He scanned her curvy body and wondered what was real and what wasn't.

Logan saw Tucker coming, and he ducked his head as if the other cowboy wouldn't see him. He had to get away before Tucker saw him talking to Layla, but his brain had taken a serious vacation.

Thankfully, a ripple went through the crowd, causing both Layla and Logan to turn. He thought perhaps Rae had come out in her wedding dress, but no. It was simply a car that had pulled up to the circle drive. Then Logan saw Sam.

He practically pushed aside wedding guests to get to the sidewalk. He half-jogged, half-walked to his brother, where he embraced him. "You made it."

"It's been rough." Sam clapped Logan on the back and stepped back. He drew Bonnie to his side, and Logan hugged her too.

"How's Boyfriend?"

"You didn't even ask me about my dog," Sam said.

Bonnie laughed. "Boyfriend is fine. He gets along great with Girlfriend."

"I guess that's what you want, right?" Logan stepped with them as they moved toward the wedding party. "I mean, I don't have a girlfriend, but if I did, I'd want to get along with her." He mentally commanded himself to stop talking. He cut a glance in Layla's direction and caught her watching him.

Or them. Maybe she was glad to see Bonnie again. Logan looked away. "I'll go tell Ben you're here." He strode toward the supply shed, his face hotter than the temperature called for. He wiped the sweat from under his hatband and determined not to look for Layla once he returned to the wedding.

CHAPTER
TWO

ayla drank too much almond punch. Ate too many parsley potatoes. Enjoyed her slice of cheesecake and half of Hazel's, who'd had to leave before dessert was served. Now that the dancing had started, Layla sat at her table with only one other woman, who watched the dance floor with her back to Layla.

She wanted to get out of her heels. Change out of this tight dress. Put on pajamas and snuggle up with a cup of coffee and her beloved black lab, Sweet Pea. She wondered how long she had to stay, and she glanced around to see if anyone else was making their way toward the parking lot.

No one seemed to be. Couples danced, and mingled, and chatted, and laughed. She'd thought the ceremony lovely and heartwarming, and she'd even felt herself tearing up at the absolute adoration Ben wore on his face for Rae.

Layla had shut those soft emotions away as quickly as

possible. She didn't have it in her to invest her time or energy into a man. Not again. Not until she figured out how to be a little less Layla and a little more…whoever it was men wanted these days.

"Do you want to dance?" a man asked, and Layla's first instinct was to say "No, thank you," without even checking to see who it was.

But she glanced up into the face of Logan Buttars, and her entire attitude changed. "Sure." She put her phone near the center of the table and stood. Her feet screamed at her to *take off these strappy heels*, so she did.

"Those shoes are killing me," she said as he looped her arm into Logan's. It was at that moment that she realized the man next to her wasn't Logan, but his twin Darren. The charcoal gray cowboy hat should've been her clue, as Logan always wore white.

Disappointment cut through her, though Darren was handsome and kind. He was quiet and straight-faced where Logan was funny and easy-going. But Layla liked him well enough to dance with him.

He just wasn't Logan.

In fact, Layla didn't see Logan again for the rest of the night, though she stayed on the dance floor for the next forty-five minutes. It seemed that all it took to get men's tongues loose was one brave person to get her out of her seat.

Layla admitted to herself that she'd had fun, and she was grateful Darren had asked her to dance. As she drove home, she lectured herself.

"You're not interested in Logan Buttars."

She put on her blinker to turn onto Main Street. She lived several blocks south, in an apartment building with a balcony that allowed her the freedom to think.

"You're not." She inched along Main Street, as everyone seemed to be out tonight. "Three dates, Layla. No one gets more than three dates."

And two years ago, when the Buttars brothers had moved to Island Park to work at Steeple Ridge Farm, Layla had seriously considered ditching her Three Date Rule for the handsome, quirky Logan Buttars.

She'd shut that down quickly too. Shut *him* down, as she'd seen the edge of interest in his eyes whenever he looked at her. She'd told herself it was for the best, that she still didn't know how to be someone she wasn't, and Logan surely wouldn't be interested in the Layla Guyman she currently was.

Then he'd started volunteering at Paw & Claws, and she was able to have her innocent daydreams about him a couple times a week. Not only that, but he was as good as she'd first supposed him to be. Went to church every week. Had a special way with animals. Chose to take the therapy dogs to the elementary school when he could've just worked around the clinic.

She pulled into the underground parking. "You're not going out with him."

He wasn't going to ask anyway. She'd made sure of that two years ago. She'd stopped lecturing herself out loud by the time she got to her apartment. Thankfully. She didn't need someone getting on the elevator and wondering who she was talking to.

Sweet met her at the door, an orange ball in his jaws. "Hey, Sweet Pea. How are you? Did you have a good night?" She scrubbed the dog along her jaw, behind her ears, and down her body. "You did, I bet. Laid around and slept, right? You lucky dog." She grinned at Sweet and headed into the kitchen to start the coffee.

The dog came with her and wound through her legs like she was part feline. Layla laughed at her and told her to get out of the kitchen. Sweet obeyed, and Layla got out a piece of dried liver for her. "What should we watch tonight?"

Sweet didn't give her opinion. She never did, and Layla ended up picking a romantic comedy she'd watched multiple times before. She changed into her pajamas while the opening scenes ran, sipped her cream-filled coffee, and let Sweet settle next to her on the couch. It was the perfect evening. The perfect evening if Layla liked having a one-sided conversation with herself and her dog.

———

THE NEXT MORNING, LAYLA ARRIVED AT PAWS & CLAWS before anyone else. She expected Hazel Long, the secretary who kept everyone on track, to arrive any minute, along with Aria Holmes. They carpooled together, worked the same hours, even shared a house on the eastern edge of town, just outside of town on the last street before the highway went on for a few miles to the farm.

Layla was friends with both of them, but she often felt like the third wheel on a bicycle when just the three of them went out. In fact, Layla felt like that a lot, as her other set of friends lived next door—and were married to each other.

She unlocked the clinic and went into her office, a sense of calm coming over her. This feeling was why she'd never left Island Park. She came to town five years ago, and she was only going to stay for one year. Get the experience she needed to work in a bigger clinic back in Boston, where her family lived.

But the charm of Island Park had infected her from the beginning, and she'd ended up buying an apartment and making roots for herself in town.

"Mornin'."

Layla turned to find Logan standing in her office doorway. Her heart thumped and pumped. She told herself to *act her age,* and said, "Morning, Logan." She leaned her hip against her desk and half-sat. "I never saw you again at the wedding."

His face went blank, and a hint of color crept from under his collar. "Yeah, I…I was around."

Layla didn't know what to do with that, so she simply continued to look at him.

"Am I taking Ginger and Bones again today?"

"If you can get Ginger Ale to go, then yes. She should go with Bones until she can go on her own."

Logan ducked the brim of his cowboy hat and straightened before walking away. Layla's heart pinched at his departure, and she sighed as she sat behind her desk. She pulled a folder she'd recently started toward her and opened it.

Her skeleton plan for a client Christmas festival sat before her. She wanted to do something for the pets and pet owners of Island Park. Something to say *thank you for trusting me with your animals*. Something that would be iconic, maybe something that could become a tradition for Paws & Claws.

She'd already outlined an animal Santa look-alike contest, and an elf pond for the kids. The third item on her list was a sleigh ride with Santa, and she tapped the tip of her pen against the paper, her mind churning.

A sleigh ride required horses, and she could only think of one place to get trained horses that would remain calm around a large crowd. Steeple Ridge Farm.

Which meant the perfect man to play Santa was Logan Buttars.

Layla's smile came instantly. She scratched out some notes just as Aria poked her head in and said, "Boy George is here."

"Be right there." She finished her sentence and slapped the folder closed, her smile still stuck in place.

"What's so happy-making?" Aria asked, finishing her second pigtail braid and using a clear elastic on the end of her sun-streaked brown hair.

"I just had the perfect idea for our Christmas celebration."

"Oh yeah?" Aria handed Layla the folder containing Boy George's medical records, and they walked down the hall together. "Would it have anything to do with the dozens of men you danced with last night?"

Layla tipped her head back and laughed. "Dozens of men? Come on."

"Once Darren got you out on the floor, you never sat down." Aria arched her left eyebrow, open curiosity on her face.

"It doesn't have anything to do with any of them." Layla knocked and entered the room, where an overly energetic Belgian Malinois—Boy George—leapt toward her, nose sniffing. She managed to shelve her thoughts of Logan during her appointments, but she secretly kept track of what time it was, knowing he'd return from the elementary school before lunch.

Her stomach growled at the same time Logan walked in the door, two dogs right at his heels. Ginger Ale was a German shepherd rescue that had come to Paw & Claws last year. Layla had recognized her gentle nature immediately, and she wanted her to work with the special needs students at the elementary school as part of her healing.

She wouldn't go without Bones, a pure white Labrador retriever who wore a smile for everyone and anyone. Sometimes Layla took Bones home to play with Sweet Pea, because the two dogs couldn't be more alike.

"Hey there," she said, her voice falsely bright. She scolded herself for speaking in such a way and went back to her adoption paperwork.

"You should've seen Ginger today. She was a real star."

Layla looked up again. Looked up, right into Logan's beautiful, dark eyes. Her mind blanked for a moment, and she remembered why she'd liked him so much from the very first time she'd seen him at church. He and his brothers all sat together, and now Rae had joined their row on the right, in the back.

"Do you have a minute?" he asked.

"Yeah." The word was made more of air than actual voice.

"You know that old barn on the south edge of town?"

"Yeah, I live near there." Thankfully she'd schooled her voice back to normal.

Logan edged a little closer, definitely closer than he'd dared before. His leg brushed hers, and she fumbled the pen across the paperwork. "Maybe you'd meet me there on Saturday. There's supposed to be a harvest picnic-something-or-other. Darren was light on the details."

Layla could barely breathe, what with Logan's cologne infusing the air around her. "So you and Darren are going?" she managed to ask.

"He mentioned it."

If she met him there, and he was with his brother…that wouldn't count as Date Number One. Layla had some specific rules for what constituted a date, and meeting somewhere rarely made the cut.

"What time?" she asked.

"You know, I'm not sure."

Layla grinned at him and dropped her eyes back to her task. Classic Logan. He was more of a big picture type of guy. Picnic, check. Time of picnic? Not so much.

"Can I text you?" he asked.

"Sure." She checked a box. "I don't have to work this weekend, so I should be free." And if she had anything on her calendar, she'd clear it. After all, a free date with Logan Buttars shouldn't be missed.

"I need your number," he said.

Layla startled and glanced down the counter. "My phone's here somewhere…."

"You don't know your number?"

"Oh, duh. Yeah, I know my number." She rattled it off for him, and he tapped it into his phone. A few moments later, her phone chimed from somewhere in the room. He touched the top of his phone to the brim of his cowboy hat, grinned, and said, "That was me."

Layla couldn't help smiling back. She leaned into the stainless steel bench and let herself get lost for a few moments. Her phone rang, jerking her from her daydream. "I should get that." She located her phone sitting near the door, where she didn't remember leaving it, and saw Meredith's name.

Logan ducked out the door just as Layla said, "Hello?"

"Hey, Lay. Are you working Saturday?"

"Nope."

"Great, there's this farmer's market—"

"But I'm busy."

Meredith paused like she didn't know the meaning of the word "busy." She inhaled, but Layla said, "There's a picnic at the old Tonic Barn."

"There is?"

"That's what—" Layla went mute, her mind oscillating between telling her best friend and keeping the fact that Logan had basically asked her out to herself. Like a delicious secret she didn't want to share with anyone quite yet.

"—I heard," she finished. She *had* heard it. She wasn't exactly lying.

Clicking came through the line, and Layla rolled her eyes. "Are you looking it up?"

"Yes, just a minute," Meredith muttered, and Layla went back to her paperwork. She'd finished two adoptions before Meredith said, "Look at that. It's the hundred-and-seventy-fifth anniversary of the Tonic Barn. The Sellers are even coming back to paint over the letters again, and there's a celebratory picnic, which starts at eleven and concludes when the painting starts at one p.m. Anyone can pay a small fee and paint a section of the barn. Huh."

"Sounds fun, right?" When she'd arrived in Island Park, Layla had been greeted by the Tonic Barn, one of the oldest buildings in Island Park. Almost two centuries ago, Preston Sellers had painted "The Woman's Tonic: Dr. Horton's Prescription" on the side of the barn as an advertisement. He or one of his ancestors had been coming back every decade or so to repaint the letters.

"That does sound fun," Meredith said, and Layla experienced a moment of panic that perhaps she and Danny would change their plans and come to the picnic. Then she'd see Layla with Logan.

Why did Layla care about that? She was friends with Logan. They spent time together at the clinic; they spoke at church; she'd never tried to hide any of those interactions.

Maybe meeting at the barn was a date.

"We could do the farmer's market in the morning," Layla said. "Is it up in Burlington?"

"Yep. They're going to have the last of the blackberries for the season."

"Sounds great," Layla said with as much forced enthusiasm as she could. "I'll bring Sweet."

"Then we can go to the picnic."

Layla's heart plummeted to her shoes. "Well…I'm meeting someone there."

"Meeting someone?" Meredith's voice had probably alerted Sweet Pea next door. "Who?"

She took a deep breath, trying to contain the smile that crept across her face. "Logan Buttars."

CHAPTER
THREE

ogan had a love-hate relationship with autumn. He loved the crisp weather, the hint of spices in the air as people made apple cider and apple pie and apple everything they could. But he really disliked the way the sun didn't make an appearance until later in the morning and seemed to disappear by six o'clock at night. Since he worked the afternoon and evening shift at Steeple Ridge, autumn meant some of his hours took place in the dark.

Autumn also meant winter was right around the corner, and Logan definitely didn't like winter. But this week, he whistled through bringing the horses in from pasture, through scrubbing the dirt and insects from their hair, through distributing their evening meal.

Because tomorrow, he had a date with Layla.

Not really a date, he thought as he checked the barn one

last time on Friday night. Everything done, he locked up and headed into the homestead. Darren had dinner on, as evidenced by the scent of roasting chicken.

"Almost done," he said from his perch at the bar.

"Gonna go shower." Logan took the stairs two at a time to the second story of the farmhouse. He and Darren used to share the basement, but once Sam had left and Ben had moved out, they'd decided to move upstairs.

Tucker had said he'd hire two new guys though they'd only really lost Sam, but Logan hadn't heard anything about it since. He got himself cleaned up and went back to the kitchen. He almost looked around for the rest of his brothers before settling his gaze on Darren.

"Chicken and potatoes. I tried to make that asparagus the way Ben did, and it didn't work out."

"Who needs vegetables?" Logan smiled at his brother, making a snap decision. "Let's pray, because I have something to tell you, but I want to eat while I do."

Darren quirked one eyebrow at him, his dark eyes glinting with questions. Logan had *maybe* mentioned to him that Layla hadn't danced yet and looked like she needed some encouragement. Darren knew about Logan's schoolboy crush on the veterinarian—or at least he had a couple of years ago. Darren had a way of sniffing *every*thing out, no matter how tight Logan held his information.

"This about Layla?" Darren asked.

"I said I wanted to pray first."

Darren smirked but folded his arms and said grace.

Logan grabbed a plate as soon as he finished and loaded his plate with a leg and a breast, as well as enough potatoes to feed a small pony.

He sat at the table, because Sam had always insisted they eat at a proper table, like a proper family. Darren let him eat his chicken leg before looking at him.

"So it's about Layla." Logan grinned and stabbed another potato. "I asked her to meet me at the barn tomorrow for the picnic."

Darren's eyes widened and his expression darkened. "So I guess I won't go."

"No, you have to come," Logan said.

"Why?"

"I don't think she wants to be alone with me."

"More like you don't want to be alone with her." Darren pointed his fork at Logan. "You want to use me as your way out if things go bad."

Logan could barely swallow. "Could things go bad?"

"Logan." Darren shook his head and speared another piece of chicken.

"She makes me so nervous," Logan admitted. "I really like her."

"Then go with her," Darren said. "What am I? The third wheel?"

"Maybe she'll feel like that too." Logan gave a one-shouldered shrug. "Tagging along with us."

"Is that what you want her to feel like? How is that romantic?"

"I'm not going for romantic."

"You're not?" Darren took a long drink of his punch. "I'm so confused."

Logan sighed and focused on his food. "Me too." He didn't know what else to say, but something boiled beneath the surface, warning him that he shouldn't show up tomorrow without his brother.

"So we're going for casual? Is that it?"

"We're going for hanging out as friends." Logan met Darren's eye. "Does that work? I mean, you and I would go and hang out. She's just meeting us there."

"But you like her." Darren got up and took his plate into the kitchen. "Is this why you volunteer at the clinic?"

"No." Logan got up even though he hadn't finished all his food. "I volunteer at the clinic because I like it. I did it in Reno too, remember?"

Darren conceded the point but wouldn't release Logan from his gaze. "So what's the code word?"

"I don't know," Logan said as if he hadn't thought about it.

His brother scoffed. "Something you don't like. Something we can work into a conversation. Something that's common."

"Pumpkin pie," Logan said.

"It's September."

"We can be creative." Logan threw his paper plate in the trashcan. "Besides, I'm not planning on using the code word to escape." He grabbed Darren's shoulders and gave his brother a little shake. "It's Layla Guyman."

"Maybe *she'll* need a code word to get away from you," Darren muttered, and Logan laughed.

"It'll be fun," he said, but Darren simply said, "Yeah, yeah," and headed for the living room to watch television.

———

Logan wasn't sure why he'd thought meeting Layla was a good idea. He'd barely been able to sleep, and he'd done all the morning chores with Darren on an empty stomach because he couldn't eat.

He'd texted Layla days ago about the start time, and he and Darren pulled into the parking lot a couple of blocks away from the barn with exactly enough minutes to spare for the walk over.

His heart pulsed against his breastbone, and he couldn't seem to get a proper breath. Clouds littered the sky, and the temperature was cool enough for a jacket but Logan hadn't brought one.

He started glancing around for Layla when they crossed Hummingbird Way and entered the old farmland. He expected her to be wearing something bright and beautiful, the way she was. So he didn't see her until she practically jumped into his arms.

"Hey, guys." She tucked her hands into her jacket pockets.

The form fitting black jacket was paired with a pair of black jeans, both of which made Logan's mind slow. The only color he could find resided on her lips, cheeks, and feet. All pink. She was stunning, even without the bright colors.

He grinned at her, realizing he hadn't even said hello yet. "Hey, Layla."

"Layla." Darren leaned in and gave her a quick hug. Jealousy soared through Logan, because there was no way he could do that. He'd probably breathe her in softly, and sigh, and slip his fingers into hers.

And that would be way too obvious. Totally out of the friend zone.

"Are you going to paint the barn?" she asked as they started wandering toward a tent that had been set up.

"Is that possible?" Logan hadn't actually done a whole lot of research on the event. He'd just wanted to find something that made it easy for him to hang out with Layla.

"Yes, silly." She giggled and bumped him with her shoulder. The fun, flirty vibe between them couldn't be one-sided, and Logan's whole body turned warm.

"You can pay five dollars to repaint part of the saying. Athena Sellers is here as the family representative. She's hired someone who paints barns for a living to make sure the integrity of the ad is maintained."

"Well, we're doing that," Logan said. "Right, Darren? You want to paint the barn, don't you?"

"There's nothing I'd like more," Darren deadpanned, and Logan wanted to elbow him.

"So we're doing that." He led the way under the tent and paid for all three of them to have a turn to paint part of the iconic barn. "And three picnic lunches," he added.

"Ham or turkey?"

"Guys." Logan turned to Layla and Darren. "Ham or turkey for lunch?"

"Ham," Darren said, the way Logan knew he would.

"Turkey," Layla said, the way Logan had guessed she would.

"Two turkey, one ham," he told the cashier.

She handed him three purple tickets. "Those are for the barn painting." She plucked three blue slips of paper from the table in front of her. "These are for your meal. Lunches are on the west side of this tent. Tables are set up in the field surrounding the barn." She grinned up at him. "Have fun."

"We will." He smiled and couldn't help the thrill of excitement that ran through him when he turned back to his friends. "Meals." He handed out the tickets. "Barn painting."

Layla positioned herself right next to him, close enough for him to hold her hand. Close enough for her to link her elbow through his arm. Close enough for him to get a whiff of her floral scent.

He cleared his throat and took a half-step away from her so he wouldn't reach out and touch her.

"I have a favor," she said.

"Oh, here we go," Logan joked. "You want my chips or something?" He kicked a smile at her.

She returned it but shook her head. "It's much bigger than chips."

Logan got a strange look in return, and he noticed the way she swallowed.

"So, I want to have a special celebration for the clients of the clinic."

"All right," Logan said. "So far, so good." He glanced

at Darren, who had his head tipped down so Logan couldn't see his eyes.

"I want to have a sleigh ride with Santa. So the best place to do that would be at Steeple Ridge. And I thought maybe the whole thing could be housed at Steeple Ridge, and I'm just wondering how possible that is." Her words practically tripped over each other and somewhere in there she'd started wringing her hands.

"You want to have a party at the farm?" Darren asked.

Logan met his eye. He honestly had no clue if that was possible. "You'd need to talk to Tucker," he said. "He owns the farm."

"Or Missy," Darren added.

Layla nodded, some of the anxiety draining from her expression. "I'll talk to them. I'll want to use the horses and stuff."

"We'd have to help," Darren said to Logan.

"I'd go to the party anyway."

Darren didn't seem like he would, but he didn't say as much.

"I'm glad to hear you'd go anyway, Logan," Layla said.

Logan liked the way she said his name, and he looked at her and smiled again. He wondered if his face looked as soft as his emotions were. "Oh, yeah?"

"Yeah. I—well, I need a Santa Claus to drive the sleigh, and I think you're the man for the job."

"Santa Claus?" Logan glanced from her to Darren, who started laughing. And laughing. And laughing.

"Why's he doing that?" Layla asked.

"It takes a lot to make Darren laugh," Logan said

darkly, not appreciating his brother in this moment. He also didn't want to play Santa Claus for a pet client party.

He met Layla's bright blue eyes, and his bones turned to dough. Maybe for her, he'd don the red suit and white beard.

Maybe.

CHAPTER
FOUR

Layla had never felt so foolish. Her face flamed like a summer bonfire, and she turned away from a still-chuckling Darren and a surly Logan. She'd never seen his eyes so dark and dangerous, and her dreams of providing a winter wonderland of fun for her clients evaporated right there on the old Olsen farm.

She pinched her meal ticket between her thumb and forefinger and strode toward the line of people waiting to pick up their boxed lunch. She collected hers, chose her chips, her favorite flavor of cookie—oatmeal raisin—and a cold bottle of water.

Once through the line, though, she didn't know where to go. Being alone at this picnic was worse that being there with a pair of brothers. Possibly. Possibly not. Layla wasn't sure. She knew a lot of people in town, and she'd taken two steps toward the elementary school principal and his family when Logan said, "I'll think about the Santa thing, okay?"

She spun around, unaware that he'd followed her. Her emotions teemed so near the surface she thought sure he'd see everything she was feeling with a simple glance. She looked away quickly. "Okay."

"So come sit by me and Darren."

She followed his gaze to where Dr. Farmer sat before turning back to him. "Okay."

"Sorry about the laughing," Darren said when Layla set her box next to his on the table. Logan sat across from them, where she could gaze at him every time she took a bite of her sandwich. Hope and desire nudged out the last of the foolish feelings still swimming in her, and she opened her lunch.

"So I take it that just because Logan is generally jolly, that he's not that into Christmas."

"He likes Christmas fine," Darren said.

"I like Christmas fine," Logan repeated. "I'm jolly?"

"Good-natured," Layla said with a smile before biting into her sandwich.

Logan seemed satisfied with her correction and they ate for a few minutes.

"It's the dressing up I don't like," Logan said. "I don't understand Halloween on a fundamental level, and we certainly don't need to extend it to Christmas."

Darren nodded his agreement while pure shock traveled through Layla. "You don't like Halloween?"

"Not even a little bit." Logan scowled and ripped open his chips.

"So last year, when I did that costume contest at the clinic and you said you were a bull rider...."

"Fake." A grin accompanied the word. "I just wore what I always wear."

"You won third place."

"Which should tell you how pathetic Halloween is." He tilted his head as if to make his point.

Layla didn't know how to respond. He'd won a ten dollar gift card to The Bean, and he'd seemed happy about the proceedings at the clinic. She squinted at him as if she could read his mind and see if he was faking now too.

"He's not that deep," Darren said out of the side of his mouth. "What you see is what you get with us Buttars."

"Is that right?"

"What are you guys muttering about?" Logan eyed Darren with suspicion, but Layla leaned in a little closer.

"What other secrets do you have about him?"

Darren flashed his own brilliant smile and whispered in her ear, "He'd kill me if I told you anything, but I like you Layla, so you should know that he snores. Loud."

Layla thought Logan would leap across the table and yank her and Darren apart. She gave a little laugh before she realized the dominant emotion storming in Logan's eyes was jealousy.

Jealousy.

He was *jealous*.

All her hopes soared toward the clouds. Maybe he was still interested in her. Maybe she hadn't ruined things between them because of her insane assumptions. Maybe she'd let him take her on Date Number Four.

She pulled back. Her Three-Date Rule existed for a reason, and she wasn't going to break it for just anyone.

But for Logan, she might.

"Logan, is that you?" Layla pulled herself from her mental examination of their fledgling relationship in time to see another blonde hovering behind Logan.

Willow Tyler.

Beautiful, blonde, confident Willow Tyler.

Layla's back stiffened, and a rush of Logan's jealousy jumped from him to her as he turned and stood. Willow stepped right into him and pecked him on the cheek, her words soft and her face absolutely glowing.

Layla mashed her sandwich wrapper into a tight ball and couldn't tear her eyes from the pair of them. They made a handsome couple, and Willow was all bone where Layla had a few extra pounds. Surely Logan—

"Don't worry about her," Darren said just as quietly as he had before. "Logan doesn't like her."

Layla met his eyes, but she couldn't tell if he was joking or not. "No? She's nice."

"I mean, he likes her fine. But he's not interested in *her*."

The way Darren emphasized the last word raised Layla's curiosity. "So he is interested?"

"In women? Sure."

"He doesn't date."

Darren cut a look toward Logan, who still stood with his back to them, seemingly willingly engaged in the conversation with Wonderful Willow.

"How do you know he doesn't date?"

Layla half snorted and half laughed. "Trust me, if he was dating someone—even once—I would know. News like that travels fast among the crowd of single women in Island Park."

"Interesting."

Layla wasn't sure what that meant. "Especially with you Buttars men. You're a coveted prize, you know."

Darren blinked, his expression turning blank.

"Ah, so you didn't know." Layla stuffed her trash in her brown box. "It's true. I even heard some of the nail technicians at the salon gossiping about which of the two of you would start dating next."

"It's not like we're drawin' straws," Darren said, a heavy note of disgust in his voice.

"I know that," Layla said. "Just because I like getting my nails done doesn't mean I'm adding to the gossip."

Darren harrumphed and set his fist heavily on the table, which caused Logan to turn. He wrapped the conversation up after that and sat back down, his gaze singular on his brother.

"Sorry," he said, finally looking at Layla. "Willow was asking me—never mind. Should we go paint the barn?"

Layla agreed, but only because Darren practically upturned the table in his haste to get up. She wanted to ask what Willow needed, and why Logan's face was flushed, and why Darren kept shooting daggered looks at his twin.

Instead, she swiped her paintbrush up and down along the lower leg of the second P in "prescription" with Logan at her side.

He was good at everything he did, and she kept

glancing at him to see how he held the brush. When she dropped hers for the third time, sending a skiff of white paint down her black pants, she just stared at the brush on the ground.

"I think I'm done."

"Oh, no, you're not." Logan scooped up the brush and moved behind her. He put the brush in her hand, but Layla froze. "You hold it loose, see? Between a couple of fingers." He demonstrated how his brush sort of revolved around his thumb and pointer fingers. "Let it do the work. You're too tense."

Layla sucked in a breath and got paint, old wood, and something distinctly Logan. Musky, and cottony, and a little bit horsey. She wanted to bottle up the smell of him and roll around in it.

Her face heated. Heck, her whole body hummed with warmth. Logan vacated the spot behind her and stepped back into his place in the line of painters. "You try it."

She wanted to, but she was so tense. The horrible words of her last real boyfriend had been unleashed from the prison where she normally kept them.

You're so intense, Layla. No man can keep up with you, and I'm tired of trying.

Logan hadn't said those exact things, but the verbiage was so very close, and tears pressed against Layla's resolve. She hadn't thought about Rick Hutchins in a long time, though he had defined her dating choices for a decade. It was because of Rick that Layla had invented and instituted the Three-Date Rule, and she hadn't been out on a Date Four with anyone since him.

Be…less you, he'd said.

Layla didn't know how to do that. It would help if she knew who she was, but she wasn't sure about that either. Though in Island Park, she felt like she was making strides toward knowing with every passing month.

"Are you really done?" Logan peered more closely at her, and his expression turned worried. "What's wrong, Layla?"

The tenderness in his voice made her chest tight and her breath catch.

"You don't have to paint." He dropped his own brush into a can of paint cleaner. "I'm definitely done."

She let him take her paintbrush from her, because she was still fighting those tears and didn't dare speak. He'd hear everything then.

"Darren, we're gonna go for a walk," Logan said. He put his hand on Layla's elbow and guided her away from the iconic barn. Once free from the crowd, and the chatter of the people, Layla's emotions started to clear.

Logan aligned his fingers with hers and she sucked in a breath. "Sorry," he said, sliding his hand away.

"No, it's…okay."

"Ah, she speaks." Logan grinned at her, and Layla barely bumped him with her shoulder.

"So the holding hands thing? That's okay?"

"Does it make this a date?"

"I have no idea." He put his hand in hers and held on tight. "Do you want this to be a date?"

She did. Badly. But she shook her head. She couldn't waste Date One on a boxed lunch with Logan's brother and ten minutes of painting. She wanted a lot more than that from her dates with Logan.

"So tell me what you know about this barn," he said, their hands swinging easily between them. Everything with Logan was easy. Talking to him. Looking at him. Being with him. He possessed a calming spirit Layla craved, and she found herself telling him all about Preston Sellers and the barn and the Olsen family who'd maintained the farm.

She finished with, "I heard they sold the land though. I wonder if they'll build on it."

"I hope not." Logan took a deep breath. "It's beautiful out here. I like how the town just sort of melts into the open country."

"Tell me about where you've lived," she said, realizing she'd dominated the conversation for a good fifteen minutes. And all about a barn.

"We came here from Reno," Logan started. He spoke of his time on the horse ranch there, and then one in Evanston before that, and one in Montana before that. His voice held low bass qualities that matched Layla's pulse, and she lost herself to the wonderful cadence of his words.

She realized when he paused and said, "We should get back," that she liked him a lot more than three dates' worth already. A beat of fear infected her heart, and she wondered what she could do to protect herself from this man.

He's not Rick, she told herself. He's not going to hurt you.

But Layla didn't quite believe herself. She enjoyed the silent serenity of Island Park as they made their way back to the barn. He wordlessly pulled his hand out of hers and tucked it in his pocket before they got within eyesight of anyone. With his head ducked and that white cowboy hat obscuring his face, she couldn't tell what he was thinking or feeling.

"So you'll think about Santa?" she asked.

"If you'll think about dinner with me next week."

A smile stole across Layla's face, and Logan matched it with one of his. "I guess I can do that."

"Great." Logan lifted his hand to catch his brother's attention. "I'll call you later then." He walked away, a bounce in his step she'd seen before. He really did have a positive outlook on life, and it was no wonder he had women approaching him everywhere he went.

Layla wrapped her arms around herself as a breeze kicked up, her smile simply refusing to leave. Her phone chimed, and she checked it.

Logan: Dinner on Monday? I can't wait to see you again.

Again.

Layla's brain recoiled, reconstructed the wall around her heart, reevaluated the relationship. All in a nanosecond. Her irrationality had made her cold toward him before. She took a deep breath and remembered how it had felt to hold his hand. Safe. Strong. Secure. He was all of those things, and she could be too if she'd let herself.

So she sent back, Monday is great. What do you like?

CHAPTER
FIVE

What do you like?

Logan could answer that question in so many ways.

I like you, Layla.

His left thumb twitched in time with his right pointer. He couldn't send that to her. He'd held her hand already, and he'd narrowly avoided a disaster with the painting. He wasn't sure what had gotten her so emotional, but he hoped it hadn't been him.

I like your pretty face. I like how great you are with Ginger Ale. I like—

"Tell her you like pizza and be done with it." Darren glared at him, taking his eyes off the road for a full five seconds. Their trusty truck stayed right on track, almost like it was a steed and could get them home by memory.

Logan shouldn't have read his texts out loud. "I like

pizza." He typed as he spoke and hit send before he could second-guess anything. "Is that okay?"

"Sure, who doesn't like pizza?"

He exhaled in relief and leaned his head back against the seat. "Dinner on Monday. Pizza with Layla." Logan couldn't remember the last time he'd been this happy. Content, sure. Jovial even. But he'd sort of forgotten what true happiness felt like.

"Great," Darren muttered, and Logan detected something behind the word that hadn't been there before.

"What's up?"

"Did you know the single women talk about us?"

Logan hadn't given it much thought. So he said, "I guess I hadn't considered it."

"Well, they do. While they get their hair and nails and stuff done."

"What kind of stuff?" Logan teased.

Darren gripped the wheel harder and glared at the countryside now. Logan laughed and checked his phone, but Layla hadn't sent anything else.

"Come on, Darren. The girls have always followed us. Me and you especially. Twin thing."

Darren said nothing.

"You're not seriously upset by that, are you?" Logan sobered long enough to really study his brother. He held his shoulders so tight, Logan thought he'd explode. "What's the big deal?"

Darren finally exhaled, those shoulders going down and his chest releasing. Thankfully, because Logan didn't truly trust the truck to get them home with an unconscious driver.

"Layla mentioned that the single women in town who talk about us were discussing which of us would start dating first. It's obviously you."

Logan's first reaction was to laugh and thank the Lord for his good fortune with Layla. Instead, he said, "Darren, if you wanted to go out with someone, you could. Obviously."

She exhaled in one long steady stream of breath. "Yeah, I know."

"So who do you want to go out with? We could double on Monday night."

"Yeah? You don't think Layla will mind?"

Logan hesitated only a moment before saying, "No, I don't think she'll mind. There's something about her."

"Something?"

"She's hesitant with me. Remember how she blew me off when we first moved here?"

"I remember you barked at everyone, including Rambo."

"I did not." Logan puffed out his chest. "I've never spoken unkindly to my dog."

A beat of silence passed before both brothers burst into laughter. When Logan quieted, he said, "So maybe I was moody."

"Is that what you call stomping around, ignoring Sam, and berating Ben for putting out ketchup with everything? Moody?"

"That is annoying," Logan said. "There are some things ketchup simply doesn't belong on."

Darren chuckled as he turned onto the road that would lead them to the proud, white farmhouse Logan had grown to love. He couldn't imagine living here without Darren, and he was sure Darren felt the same.

"So who are you gonna ask out?" Logan got out of the truck and whistled for Rambo, who came tearing around the side of the house.

"I don't know," Darren said. "Maybe I'll spot someone at church tomorrow."

Logan nodded as he bent down and scrubbed his dog. "Hey, bud. Should we throw a ball? Should we? Yeah, let's throw a ball."

Rambo barked his excitement, and Logan glanced around to find one of the dog's orange balls. He caught sight of Darren's back as he mounted the front steps and disappeared into the house. His twin sense fired on all cylinders, and Logan knew he'd better find a woman for Darren, stat, or there'd be a lot more barking around Steeple Ridge.

LOGAN ADJUSTED HIS PALE PINK TIE JUST BEFORE HE ENTERED the chapel. Darren followed him, and Logan set his feet toward the bench in the back where they'd sat every week for the past two years. Ben and Rae were already there, fresh off their honeymoon. Logan took one look at his youngest brother and saw the glow of joy.

His throat thickened. He wanted that joy, that companionship, that love. "Hey." He sat next to Ben and let his gaze wander the patrons already in their seats. He didn't see Layla's blonde waves, and a pang of disappointment sliced through him.

Darren sat on the end and Logan leaned toward him. "See anyone?"

"Leave me be," he growled, but Logan could tell his brother was looking. So he let him look, though he already had the perfect woman for him.

Willow Tyler.

Pastor Gray stood and invited the choir to come to the front. They sang several numbers before retaking their seats. Sam would've loved the musical performance, so Logan fired off a text to his oldest brother. He followed it with, *Going out with Layla Guyman tomorrow.*

That's great, Sam texted back. *Bonnie says to talk to Rae about Layla.*

Concern furrowed Logan's brow. *What does that mean?*

It took several minutes—several annoying minutes where Logan actually shook his phone once to make sure it was still on and receiving texts—before he got another message.

Logan, this is Bonnie. I don't know much about it, because Layla was Rae's friend, and I was Rae's friend…sort of. But I know enough that Layla doesn't date someone for very long. Something about some rules. Just ask her.

Right, Logan thought. On their first date, he was going to lead with why Layla didn't date the same person for long. And asking Rae? Out of the question.

Just because he'd told Sam and Darren about Layla didn't mean Ben and Rae needed to know. He slid a glare in Ben's direction as if he'd purposely spied on Logan's private text conversation. Of course, he wasn't even looking in Logan's direction but was focused on the pastor.

Where Logan should be centering his attention. He did, but the sermon didn't make much sense now that he'd missed half of it. He stewed over Layla, trying to remember the last guy she'd been out with. He couldn't. But she had to have gone out with someone in the past two years. Someone as beautiful and charming as her surely didn't stay home on Friday nights. Did she?

"Are you gonna do the Santa thing?" Darren asked as they stood to sing the closing hymn.

"If you ask out Willow Tyler," he whispered back. The song started, but neither brother sang.

"Willow?" Darren asked, his voice barely audible above the music.

"She's blonde. Pretty. Nice."

Darren's eyes could've cut holes in Logan, and he faced the front and started belting out the hymn. Logan rolled his eyes and stayed silent. He didn't hide his preference for blondes from his brothers, but Darren had always insisted a woman's hair color didn't matter. And of course, it didn't. But Logan knew Darren had a thing for blondes, same as him.

The service ended, and Logan nudged Darren. "She's right there."

"She's also surrounded by five other women. Leave me

be." Darren moved into the aisle and took slow steps toward the exit in the back.

"What's going on?" Ben asked.

"Nothing." Logan gave him the fastest smile possible and scanned the crowd for Layla. He'd seen her at church plenty of times. It had been a sweet kind of torture, something he wanted to endure over and over simply to be near her. Touching her had been fifty times better, and Logan had dreamt of kissing her last night.

He schooled his thoughts as he finally caught sight of her. She walked with Hazel Long, the secretary at the clinic, her face beaming with laughter. Her eyes met his, and she ducked her head in a sexy, shy way that had Logan moving in her direction. He intercepted her just as she entered the lobby. "Hey, quick question: If Darren got a date, could he come with us tomorrow night?"

She exchanged a glance with Hazel, who tucked her hair and continued toward the outside doors while Layla pulled him down the hall to her right. His skin tingled where she touched it, and he wore a smile he knew had to look goofy.

"Date?" she hissed.

"Yeah, we're goin' to get pizza tomorrow, remember?"

"We didn't define it as a date."

"Is that a problem?"

She looked over his shoulder, but Logan kept his attention on her, not wanting to miss a tick of her eye or a quick pucker of her lips. "Who's Darren going to ask?"

"I don't know. I suggested Willow Tyler, but he didn't seem too keen about that."

Her gaze wandered back to his. "Willow is not Darren's type."

"Oh no?" Logan reached for her hand, a slight movement of his fingers toward hers. He brushed them but didn't grab on. He let his arm settle at his side again. "Who is?"

"Darren needs someone who can bring him to life. Willow doesn't…it's not her. Maybe Farrah Irvine. Have you met her?"

"Her name sounds familiar. What color is her hair?"

Layla flinched the teensiest bit, like Logan had flicked water in her face. He hastened to explain that, "Darren sort of likes blondes. He'll be more receptive to the idea of someone he hasn't met if she's blonde."

"She's sort of a dark blonde." Layla peered around him, stepping right into his personal space, even going so far as to grip his bicep to steady herself as she searched the lobby. "She's right there. See?" She turned him as if he was putty in her hands, which he basically was. "By the drinking fountain. Red top."

Logan spotted her, and his heart danced the way his horse did when she didn't want to go into the river. "Oh, we've met her. She works with horses, and met us in town to get hers last winter so we could to board them."

"Her father always boards his horses at Steeple Ridge. He lives in Burlington, and owns a chain of movie theaters."

"Right, I've heard Missy talk about him."

"Farrah is his daughter. She lives here in town."

"Her last name is Irvine?"

"Married and divorced."

Logan chewed on this information while eyeing Farrah. He felt like he was sizing up a horse to see if he wanted to buy her. He shook his head to clear his thoughts. "Let's get her and Darren together."

"Where is he?"

"Probably in the truck."

"Well, that's not going to work, is it?" She marched past him and went over to Farrah. They chatted for a minute or so, and then she twisted and pointed at Logan. He lifted his hand in a half-hearted hello, wondering what Layla had said. Farrah smiled and twirled the ends of her very long caramel-blonde hair around her fingers.

Darren would like her. Logan pulled out his phone and texted Darren. *Where are you?*

Standing on the sidewalk outside.

I found you a date.

I don't want to go out with Willow.

Not Willow. Come back inside.

His brother darkened the doorway of the church only a few seconds later, and Layla latched onto him. Logan watched for approximately ten seconds before Darren glanced over his shoulder, pure desperation on his face.

Logan chuckled as he hurried over to the threesome, hoping Darren wouldn't be angry and that he'd like Farrah. One glance at his twin's face, and Logan's fears calmed.

At least until Darren leaned over and whispered, "You better suit up, Santa."

CHAPTER SIX

'll be your Santa Claus.

Layla stared at the text, wondering what had convinced Logan to play the part, to dress up as he professed to hate. She wanted to ask him, but her euphoria prevented her from doing so. She'd need to hit the planning hard when she got to the office tomorrow.

If she could even focus. The very idea of going to dinner with Logan had her whole life in a blender. "But it's not a date," she told herself as she went through the motions of putting together a chili. She loved the cooler weather, because she could get back to eating her favorite food: soup.

She half shrugged as she scooped the diced green peppers onto her knife and dropped them into the already sautéing onions, garlic, and butter.

"Half a date," she conceded. "A double date doesn't count as a full date." In her experience, a double date was almost like simply hanging out. She'd practically doubled with Logan and Darren yesterday.

"Right, Sweet?" The black lab just stared at her. "Right. It's half a date. That gives me two-and-a-half more before...." She let the sentence hang there, because the thought of cutting Logan out of her life for a second time couldn't be spoken out loud.

She chewed on the idea of eliminating her Dating Rules altogether, but she hadn't fully decided when her phone rang. It would be her mother, ready for their Sunday evening chat. Hopefully something had happened with the college student rentals she managed with Layla's two sisters. Then all Layla would have to say was, "Wow!" or "Uh huh," or "Yeah."

"Hey, Mom." She put the phone on speaker as she added the spices to her chili.

"Hey, honey. How was your week?"

Her mind flashed to the barn painting, the hand holding. "Oh, you know. Same old, same old." She smiled at her secret and reached for the can opener to get the beans in the chili.

"You wouldn't believe what we found under the bed during move-in this week."

"I'm sure I won't." Layla dumped the beans into the pot, stirred the chili, and leaned against the counter to "Mmm," and "No way!" as her mom told her about a pumpkin—a very rotten pumpkin—they'd found when the students moved in and reported a funky smell.

She asked about her sisters, Vanessa and Alice, both younger than her. Alice was still in college herself, and

Vanessa ran the registration and administrative side of their rental business. They were both "Great, and wanted me to tell you to come visit as soon as you can."

Layla smiled, her sense of belonging to her family warming a little. Since she'd decided to branch outside of the family business, Layla had felt like an outsider. They never asked her to come work with them, but Vanessa had a way of needling her about living three hours north of Boston, as if there wasn't a better city to live in.

"What about you, hon?"

"So…I might be dating someone."

"Dating? Nessa, Layla is dating someone!"

"Mom," Layla said, sighing. "I said I *might* be dating someone."

Didn't matter. Her mom didn't even hear her. Mostly because Vanessa had taken the line. "You're dating?" her sister asked. "More than three times?"

"Not even first date yet," Layla said. "Which is why I told Mom I *might* be dating someone."

"I don't understand."

"I don't either. Forget I said anything."

Vanessa scoffed, and Layla imagined her tossing her golden waves of hair over her shoulder. Layla had been dying hers whiter and whiter over the past few years in an attempt to look different from her practically perfect sister. "Right," Vanessa said. "Like I'm going to forget about you dating someone. You haven't dated in a decade."

"That's not true."

"No? Name the last man you dated."

Layla pressed her lips together, because the answer was

Rick. And they had broken up almost ten years ago. "I have Rules," Layla said.

"Are you willing to break them for this man?"

"Maybe."

"What would get you to yes?"

"I don't know," Layla admitted. "I haven't ever thought that far ahead."

"What's his name?"

"Logan."

"Oh, you're going to break your rules." Vanessa laughed, a high-pitched, pealing type of sound.

"How do you know?"

"You sighed his name like *Loooogan*."

"I did not." Layla couldn't help giggling. "I have to go. My chili is boiling."

"Wait. When are you going to see Logan again?"

"Tomorrow. He volunteers at the clinic."

"I'll expect a text then." Vanessa said it in such a way that there was no wiggle room. "Ma, she has to go. She said she had to go."

Layla enjoyed the bickering of her family in their Bostonian accents. She knew her mom would get back on the line, so she just waited while she told Vanessa, "Just give it to me. I want to talk to her again." She finally got the phone and said, "Layla, good luck tomorrow."

"Tomorrow?"

"Vanessa said you're seeing your boyfriend tomorrow."

"No, Ma, he's not—"

"Oh, your dad wants to say hello."

After turning off the stove so her chili wouldn't burn,

Layla sighed back into the counter. She shouldn't have said anything about Logan. What had she been thinking? She'd gone from half-a-date—which she hadn't even gone on yet—to having a boyfriend in the span of ten minutes.

"Layla?" At least her father wouldn't badger her about her "boyfriend."

"Hey, Dad."

"How are things at the clinic?"

Layla breathed in the normalcy of her dad, even though they didn't always get along. At least he hadn't asked about Logan, and by the time she hung up, she didn't feel so crazed. Surely she'd just given her mom and Vanessa something to gossip about for hours. Her phone chimed, and she glanced at it. Vanessa.

She growled as she muted the conversation. She could only handle so much and she wanted to be able to control when she had to deal with her sister. But she had chili, and her pile of expensive, homemade papers, and Logan on her mind, so the evening wasn't a total loss.

LAYLA POSITIONED HER ORIGAMI DOG NEAR THE LEASHES, where Logan would see it. Sure enough, he pushed through the door, his gaze first finding hers. She glanced to the dog, and he followed. "Is this for me?"

"Did you know I liked origami?" Layla bent back over her paperwork, this routine welcome. She hoped she was skilled enough at flirting, as she'd been out of practice.

"I did not know you liked origami." Logan picked up the dog and rotated it. "Is this Rambo?"

"Sure is."

He came closer and closer, her pulse accelerating with every step he took. "It's beautiful." He tucked a lock of her hair behind her ear, and the gentle skate of his fingers across her skin sent explosions through her bloodstream.

"You're beautiful." He leaned down and pressed his mouth to her cheek. "Are we still on for dinner?"

"I don't know. You tell me. Did Darren ask Farrah?"

"He called her this morning." Logan grinned and stepped back. He admired the paper dog again, and a flash of pride stole through Layla. Making the intricate folds origami required always soothed her. Being able to take something flat and make it three-dimensional, give it life, brought her joy.

"Ben is letting us borrow his car so we don't all have to squish into the truck."

Squishing next to Logan sounded fine to Layla, but she said, "Oh, that's great."

"What about lunch after I get back from the therapy?"

"I can't today. The girls and I are going to the country club."

Logan's right eyebrow quirked. "The country club? How fancy."

"They have an amazing salad bar on Mondays." She pretended to know what she was looking at on her clipboard, but Logan's proximity made working impossible.

"So you go every Monday?"

"Usually, yeah."

"I didn't know you played golf."

Layla looked up and laughed. "I don't play golf."

"How do you go to the country club then?"

"I'm a social member. It's five dollars a month, and I have to spend thirty dollars a month on food. That's it."

Logan took a few seconds to absorb her statement. "So you pay a monthly fee so you can eat at a salad bar?"

"An *amazing* salad bar," Layla corrected him. "And they're never busy. We never wait for a table. And I get two-dollar tacos on Tuesdays."

"Oh, well, then sign me up." Logan chuckled, and Layla added her giggle to his laughter.

"You can just come with me," she said. "Not every person who eats has to be a member. They just have to be with one."

"Got it." Logan backed up and reached for Bones's leash. "So you never answered me about the Santa thing. Maybe you've changed your mind?"

She laughed again. "Nice try. No, it's going to be an amazing event. Could you stay a bit longer one day this week so we can go over the details?"

"Oh, I'm not a details type of guy." Logan bent to leash Bones. "You knew that, right? I need to be bossed. You tell me where and what time to show up and I'll have the suit on."

Layla frowned. "But I was hoping we could work on it together."

Logan unlatched Ginger Ale's kennel and let her out. "Well, I can sit with you, but don't count on me to contribute much."

"Sitting with me would be fine."

"Tomorrow okay?"

"Sure." She beamed at him, and he ducked his cowboy hat in good-bye as he led the dogs out the door and to their therapy sessions.

———

LAYLA PACED THE LENGTH OF HER HOUSE. DOWN THE HALL, touch the linen closet, turn, go all the way to the front door, touch, spin, repeat.

Logan was late.

He'd texted to say they'd be late, as Rae hadn't quite been home from work when they showed up to borrow the car. Layla wasn't sure why her stomach was so angry. She'd spoken to Logan that day. He'd taken Rambo-the-paper-dog home with him. He'd kissed her cheek.

"That's why," she muttered as she wrung her fingers. "What if he tries to kiss you tonight?"

Kissing on the mouth automatically catapulted a man into the boyfriend category. Rule Number Six said so. Layla didn't have a lot of experience with any of the Rules after the first, because the first said she had to break things off after the third date. She hadn't broken that one yet, and she'd never needed any of her other rules.

In her experience, kissing happened on Date Four, which was why she set the cutoff at three. Then she didn't have a boyfriend. There didn't have to be messy breakups. She didn't have to wonder if she'd just been "less her" if things would've work out.

She was in control with the Three Date Rule. And she liked that.

With Logan, though, she felt very out of control. Tonight could technically be counted as Date Two, and she was nowhere near ready to stop seeing him.

"But it's not Date Two." She touched the linen closet. Turned. "It's Date One-Half. Double dates only count as half."

Her doorbell chimed, and she half-shrieked half-sucked in a breath. The result was torture on her throat, and she coughed. She couldn't answer the door coughing and with a throat on fire. She stepped to the kitchen sink and got a glass of water. She'd just gotten her coughing controlled when the doorbell rang again. Logan knocked this time too. Loud.

"Coming!" she called as she swept her purse off the counter and hurried toward the door. She pulled it open to the gloriously handsome face she'd been dreaming about for a long time. Maybe even before she realized who it belonged to. "Hey."

"Hey, yourself." He scanned her, his smile lingering. "Wow, a dress and everything."

"I wear dresses to work."

"Rarely," he said, and she wondered how long he'd been keeping track of her wardrobe choices. He leaned in her doorway and snaked his hand around her waist so he could place a kiss on her forehead. "But I like it. You look great in navy blue. Something about that dark color and the whiteness of your hair."

"It's fake, by the way."

"What? The hair?"

"Totally fake. Right out of a bottle."

He looped the end of a strand around his finger. "Hmm." He gazed down at her with more heat in his eyes than ten summers full of sun. "I wonder what else is fake about you."

Feeling brave, and bold, and flirty, and fun, Layla reached up and touched his bicep. "I was wondering the same thing, but nope. Those muscles are real."

He tipped his head back and laughed. "I work hard for these."

"Right," she said. "Lifting straw and hay and manhandling horses."

"I do not manhandle horses." He hadn't given her an inch to breathe, and she felt one second from passing out. "They listen to me. All I do is cluck my tongue or snap my fingers, and they follow me."

"Sure," she said, her brain misfiring.

He held her close, right there in her doorway. Anyone could walk out of their apartment and see them. Layla found she didn't care. Maybe it was time to let everyone in Island Park know Logan Buttars was off the market.

CHAPTER
SEVEN

Logan experienced the drawn-out moments between him and Layla. His mind revolved around kissing her, and kissing her now. But something held him back—and it wasn't the way Layla was stroking her fingers down the buttons on his shirt.

"Should we go?" she asked.

"Sure," he said, taking a step out of her doorway and lacing his fingers through hers. "Darren is probably spitting fire by now."

"Oh yeah? Why?"

"He's not the world's greatest conversationalist."

"You mean compared to you."

"I *am* great at small talk," Logan said with a smile. "Darren usually just hovers nearby and I get us dates." He realized too late what he'd said. "I mean—I used to. You know, before moving here."

"Why haven't you dated since you moved here?"

Logan bit back the words he wanted to say. *Because you wouldn't go out with me.* He hadn't even realized how deep his crush on Layla had been until Saturday. The need to know why she'd put the brakes on their relationship all those months ago writhed under his skin. But he wasn't going to ask her. He wanted to, but Darren said to give it a few dates. Logan hoped there would be a lot more than a few.

"So, tell me about your family." He reached out and pushed the call button for the elevator.

"Oh, that's a zoo waiting to happen."

"Well, you've seen the Buttars Disaster, so I'm sure I can handle it."

"My dad is a professor at Boston University." She stepped on the elevator when it arrived, and Logan followed her. He crowded right next to her, his fantasies running wild again. Thankfully, she continued speaking and Logan focused on her words so he wouldn't press her against the wall and kiss her. Oh, how he wanted to kiss her.

"My mom and two sisters own and manage a student housing development just off campus. Over two hundred students live there from September to May."

"Oh, wow."

"Like I said. A zoo."

"I never went to college." Logan's voice held a hollow note. "My parents died only a few months after Darren and I graduated from high school. We—" He cleared his throat. "We were going to go, but then Sam took us to the ranch in Montana where he was working. I love horses, so it was okay with me."

Her hand tightened on his. "I'm sorry about your parents."

A ghost of a grin crossed his face. "Me too. They were great people. They would've liked you."

"Oh yeah? How do you know?"

"My momma loved dogs. At one point I think we had five or six strays she put food out for. Drove my dad nuts." Logan chuckled and stepped into the lobby of Layla's apartment building. His stomach felt shredded, and not even the thought of sausage and bacon and marinara sauce could quell it.

"I'm thinking about going to school to get my veterinary technician license."

Her eyebrows shot up. "That's great, Logan. You should really do that."

"Or I was thinking of maybe learning how to train therapy dogs." Everything inside him spun out of control. He hadn't shared any of this with anyone, not even Darren. "I think I'm good at handling dogs, and I love seeing how they help kids, veterans, and disabled people." He shrugged. "Maybe I could train hospital therapy dogs and really help people."

Layla gazed at him with a measure of adoration in her eyes. He felt unworthy of it, as he hadn't even looked into how to become a service dog trainer. His thoughts were big and bold, and he rarely delved into the details.

But for this, he might. He liked working at Steeple Ridge, but his true love laid with dogs, not horses, and his time at the elementary school with Bones and Ginger Ale was the highlight of his week.

"I think you should definitely do that," she said. "You'd be great in a clinic, but you belong with dogs in a hospital, or a school, or in someone's home." She nodded, a small smile spreading her lips. "You do."

She left her hand in his as they exited the building, and Logan met his brother's eyes. Sure enough, Darren looked like he could commit manslaughter, and Logan knew he was his brother's target.

"Uh oh," Layla whispered. "He doesn't look happy."

"You think he doesn't like Farrah?"

"That would be impossible."

Logan opened the door behind Farrah and let Layla settle in the car before rounding the back of the car and sliding into the backseat with her. Layla was already chatting with Darren, asking him about Paintbrush, his prized horse. A flood of appreciation flowed through him, and he flashed her a grateful grin.

Darren put the car in gear and took them out of the underground parking garage. He gave Layla answers, and Farrah joined in the conversation about Steeple Ridge and the horses there.

"You should come out," he said. "We could ride together until the weather turns bad."

"Oh, I don't know." Farrah fiddled with the bell sleeves on her shirt. "I haven't been out to Steeple Ridge in a while."

"That's not true," Darren said. "You came last winter to board six horses."

"We met in town," Farrah said as Logan cringed and looked out the window. Darren was too obvious in his memories of Farrah. But he hadn't said anything to Logan about her.

Darren glanced at her while stopped at a four-way stop. "Right? I mean, that's what Logan said."

Good save, Logan thought.

"Yeah, we've boarded at Steeple Ridge for years," Farrah said. "I mean I don't ride anymore."

"Why not?"

"I don't know," Farrah said, but Layla said, "She was a champion jumper."

"Layla," Farrah chastised. "I don't ride anymore." She spoke to Darren. "I haven't been back to Steeple Ridge to ride. That's what I meant."

"All right," Darren said and he dropped the subject. He didn't have the liberty to watch Farrah, but Logan did, and he saw the blush enter her face. Saw her cut Layla a dirty look. Saw her glance at Darren, and Logan saw the interest in her eyes.

He grinned as Darren parked behind the pizza parlor. If Darren could keep himself from saying something to make Farrah uncomfortable, this could be a great date for everyone. In order to keep his brother comfortable, he didn't reach for Layla's hand though he desperately wanted to. She seemed to get the hint, because she walked right next to Darren and engaged both him and Farrah in another conversation, this one about the upcoming Witch Festival at Howland Park, somewhere Logan had never heard of.

———

LOGAN WHISTLED THROUGH THE NEXT SEVERAL DAYS. HE worked with the horses, and threw a ball to Rambo, and completed his special needs therapy. He saw Layla at work when he'd gone in on Thursday, but she'd been engaged in a conversation with Hazel. She'd caught his eye and smiled, and he'd texted her enough to require a new cell phone plan with more minutes.

But he hadn't seen her again. Hadn't been able to hold her hand or smell her perfume. He thought he might be able to get into town on Saturday, but Tucker had asked Darren and Logan to help the new cowhands move in.

Thankfully, the weather had cooled enough that hauling boxes and mattresses didn't make Logan break a sweat. The moving in only took about an hour, and then Logan turned on the grill and got out the ground beef.

One of the new guys, Wade, joined him on the back patio. He swiped off his cowboy hat and gazed out at the barns. "This sure is a nice place."

"You haven't been here before?" Logan wasn't all that surprised. Sam had brought them here, sight unseen.

"Nope. Cody and I just picked up the job when it came on the board. Hadn't been to Vermont yet."

"You'll like it here," Logan said. "Tucker and Missy are great bosses, and the work is good."

Cody's footsteps crunched on the gravel on the west side of the house, and he came around the corner with a dog. Logan eyed Rambo and said, "No. Stay." His dog stayed but a whine pitched into the air as the other animal came closer.

"Beautiful golden retriever," Logan said. "What's his name?"

"This is Honey," Cody said. "Sit." The dog sat, her tongue lolling out of her mouth and the happiest look on her face. Logan loved golden retrievers, and he wondered if Rambo would be able to keep up with her.

"Lunch will be ready in a minute."

"We don't work weekends?"

"Darren and I took care of almost everything this morning." Logan put the burgers on the grill and closed the lid. "And Tucker and Missy are taking this afternoon. It's rare we get this much time off." He moved to the picnic table and climbed on top of it. "I'm gonna enjoy it."

Wade and Cody didn't say much else, and that was just fine with Logan. He leaned back on his elbows and closed his eyes, aware of when Cody picked up a ball and threw it for the dogs. He smiled, the weak autumn light falling across his face welcome and warm.

He'd been dreading the arrival of the new cowhands, but as Cody whistled through his teeth and both dogs came tearing back to him, Logan decided having new men in the house wouldn't be so bad after all.

The next day, Logan's heart stutter-stepped the way his horse did when it didn't want to get in the trailer. Darren parked the truck in the lot at the red brick church and got out without a backward glance at Logan. Within a few steps, Farrah joined him and though Logan could only see half of his brother's face as he turned toward her, he found the happiness easily.

If only he could just sidle up to Layla like that. Everything had always seemed so much easier for his brothers than for him. Even though he was the most easy-going of the lot, things certainly didn't seem to go easy for him.

He wanted to sit by Layla, but he hadn't brought it up and she normally sat with Hazel and a couple other girls from the clinic. Logan wanted to throw a giant wrench into her routine, but he didn't want to disrupt the flow they had going. After all, Layla didn't seem to like disruptions.

So he got himself out of the truck and into the church. He ducked into the chapel and pressed his back into the wall as he scanned who'd already come in and taken their seats. Ben and Rae had claimed their spot in the corner. Darren stood at the end of the aisle, talking to Farrah.

Logan watched them for a moment, wondering if she'd sit with the family already. Darren had always been a no-nonsense type of dater. If he liked a woman, he went out with her. If he didn't, he didn't bother. He wasn't one to prolong things, or wait to see how things shook out.

"Hey."

Logan jumped at the feminine voice, so deep in his thoughts as he was. He glanced at the woman who'd stopped next to him, and everything inside him relaxed. "Layla."

"Who are you looking for?"

"You." Logan groaned inwardly, wishing he'd been able to censor himself a little quicker. "I mean, I thought...." He wasn't quite sure what he'd been thinking.

It seemed a bit premature to sit together at church, and the only other thing he could thing of was inviting her to the family dinner that evening at the farmhouse. But it was beyond too early for that. He should probably kiss the woman first, and once he thought that, he couldn't seem to think about anything else. His eyes dropped to her mouth and his throat turned to sand.

"Seems like Darren and Farrah are getting along."

"He said he had a good time last night."

"Did you have a good time last night?" Layla nudged him with her shoulder.

Logan's blood ran a little hotter and a flush crept into his face. "Of course. Best pizza I've ever had."

She giggled and shook her head. "The anchovies were a joke."

"I ate them, didn't I?"

"You looked like you were going to throw up."

"I'm going to put that twenty bucks to good use."

"Oh yeah? What are you going to do with it?"

With the easy banter, and the way her floral perfume infected his sense of smell, Logan's confidence grew at the same rate his anxiety lessened. He slipped his hand into hers. "Take you to the movies in Burlington."

"Is that right?"

Logan wouldn't look at her, and he kept their joined hands concealed behind his body. "Will you go with me? I'll drive, and you can pick the movie."

"Dinner too?"

"If you'd like."

"Your twenty won't cover that."

"I have more money." Logan feigned nonchalance, but inside, his pulse bounced from his throat to his chest to the top of his skull.

Hazel entered the chapel and headed down the left side aisle to a row in the middle of the congregation. Layla pulled her hand away from Logan's, said, "All right. Friday night?" and looked at him.

Logan catalogued the hope in her eyes, the beauty in the lines of her face, the goodness in her soul.

"Friday night," he confirmed, finally able to move away from the wall when she walked down the aisle and took her seat with her friends.

CHAPTER
EIGHT

Layla fretted over breakfast on Monday. And Tuesday. And Wednesday. She couldn't enjoy her nighttime routine of trying a new soup recipe and relaxing in front of the TV as it played a romantic comedy.

There could be no relaxing when a date—a real, single date with the very alive, single Logan Buttars—sat on the horizon. Taunting her and her Dating Rules.

"What are you going to do now?" she'd muttered to herself on more than one occasion. Once while she wasn't alone, and the conversation with Aria, her veterinary technician, didn't go well. Aria had known something was up —way up—and when she entered Layla's office near closing time on Wednesday, she had Hazel with her.

They took the two available chairs across from Layla's desk and looked at each other for a long moment. Then they simultaneously switched their gaze to Layla, whose heart raced like she'd just finished a marathon. "What's going on with you and Logan Buttars?" Aria asked.

Layla deliberately set down her pen on their last client of the day. "We've been…seeing each other." That wasn't a lie. She did see him. But she wasn't dating him. She wouldn't say that. In fact, being able to deny dating was the reason she had the Dating Rules.

"When are you 'seeing him' again?" Hazel tossed her abnormally long hair over her shoulder.

"Tomorrow night." Layla leaned her elbows on her desk and decided to lay everything out. Get some help. She certainly needed it. "It's our first official date alone. The one where we met at the Tonic Barn for lunch didn't count. His brother came with him. And we went to the Pizza Palace on Monday night last week, but this time Darren brought a date."

"So you've already been out with him twice?" Hazel's shocked tone seemed to catch in the corners of the office. "So tomorrow night, it's over. Is that it?"

"No." Layla shook her head. "No. Meeting someone for a boxed lunch with their brother doesn't count as a date."

"Technicality," Aria muttered out of the side of her mouth, but Layla ignored her.

"And a double date only counts as half." She lifted her chin in defiance. "So tomorrow night makes one and a half dates."

"Halfway there," Hazel said. "What are you going to do when it gets to three? Or will you cut him off at two and a half?" She looked at Aria. "I mean, she can't go to three and half with him. Right? So she gets tomorrow night and then one more date."

"Or two more doubles," Aria said, and the way they talked about her like she wasn't even there annoyed Layla to no end.

"Maybe I won't cut him off at three dates," Layla said to get them to stop speaking.

Hazel blinked at her, her mouth hanging slightly open.

"So you like him," Aria said with a knowing tone. "She really likes him," she said to Hazel.

Layla moaned and put her head in her hands. "I really like him."

"You've liked him for two years," Hazel finally said. "This is two years of repressed feelings finally coming to the surface." She sucked in a breath and held it. "Oh, I just thought of something. Have you already kissed him?"

Layla lifted her head as if someone had shot it out of a cannon. "No. No kissing until Date Four."

"Which is why you never get to Date Four." Aria gave her a pointed look that stabbed all the way through Layla's chest.

"I bet the fireworks between you two are amazing." Hazel sighed in a wistful way, and a pang of regret hit Layla. Hazel wanted to date. Wanted to find someone. Hadn't been asked out in probably three months.

"You know he's liked you for two years too," Aria said.

Layla's gaze flew to her friend's. She'd always admired Aria's cute pixie cut, her wide, brown eyes. "He has? How do you know?"

"He told me once."

Shock traveled through Layla in powerful waves.

"I mean, he didn't come right out and say it." Aria lifted one shoulder like what she was saying wasn't the most earth-shattering thing on the planet. But to Layla it was.

"But I asked him about being a bachelor for one of our Maple Days fundraisers, and he said he wasn't interested in that kind of thing."

"So what?" Hazel asked. "That doesn't mean he's liked Layla for two years."

"Then Layla came into the back room where he was getting the dogs ready, and his whole face lit up. He turned back to me and asked if Layla would bid on the bachelors. I said, no, she doesn't normally do stuff like that." Aria gave a small laugh as she relived the moment right there in front of them. "He looked like I'd just told him there would be no Christmas that year, and he skulked out with a grumbly look on his face."

"Skulked?" Hazel's loud laugh actually hurt Layla's ears. "Who talks like that?"

"I've never seen Logan look grumbly either," Layla said, absolutely refusing to believe that Logan had liked her all this time. All this time she'd been harboring secret daydreams about him. All this time she'd been wondering if she'd ever break her Three Date Rule for a man, and who that would be.

Could it be Logan?

Why not? she thought.

Is it Logan? she asked, tilting her head toward heaven. God had never truly directed her in matters of the heart, but she supposed she hadn't exactly given Him a chance. She hadn't given herself a chance.

"He's only been volunteering at the clinic for what?" Hazel looked at Layla. "A year?"

"He started in January," Layla said. "So almost two years." A slow burn started in her toes and worked its way upward. "And we were friendly right when he moved to town. He asked me to show him around town, and I got scared, and…." She let her words fade into silence, because she didn't want to speak them. Didn't want to vocalize out loud that she'd already employed her dating rules on him, but after only one date instead of her usual three.

Maybe you knew then, she told herself. And you weren't ready.

But the million-dollar question now couldn't be avoided. Was she ready to break her rules and give herself a chance at love now?

———

THE NEXT DAY, LAYLA HAD JUST SHOVELED A FORKFUL OF greens, almonds, and avocado into her mouth when Logan knocked on her open door and then leaned into the doorframe in the sexiest way possible. She almost choked but managed to chew and swallow.

"What are you doing here?" she asked, stirring her salad without the intention of taking another bite.

"You asked me to stay after the therapy today, remember? You blew me off last week?"

She rose from her desk. "I did not blow you off. I was busy."

Logan kicked a sultry smile in her direction. She wished it didn't dive straight into the fleshy parts of her heart and make her want to abandon all the carefully planned rules she'd constructed to protect herself.

He won't hurt you. It was the second time she'd had that thought, and she wondered if it was coming from her or from a higher power.

"Maybe you don't want to do the Christmas party anymore," he said.

"Of course I do." She pushed her salad to the side and pulled her folder from the desk drawer where she'd placed it earlier this week. "Come on in. Sit down."

"I didn't mean to interrupt your lunch."

"It's a salad."

"That's what you like for lunch, right?" Logan watched her in an even, calm way that unnerved her.

"Right." She cleared her throat, wishing she could really eat pizza and pasta for every meal. But she already carried those fifteen extra pounds, and she did like avacadoes so she didn't feel too deprived.

She flipped open the folder. "So I was thinking it would be a winter carnival." She gazed at the drawing she'd done over the weekend. She hadn't wanted to meet with Logan last week, because the truth was she wasn't ready. It had been an exceptionally busy week in the clinic, and she'd done most of the work for this at home.

She slid the map over to him. "So it would be staged at Steeple Ridge. Have you talked to Tucker and Missy?"

"Yeah." Logan looked at the map. "Ice skating, elf pond, reindeer ring toss." He glanced up at her. "You even drew in a little Rudolph." The grin he gave her spoke of how much he liked her. If only a stab of fear didn't drive right through her heart.

"There's a hot chocolate express, and of course, pictures with Santa."

"And the sleigh ride with Santa," she said. "I want to see you in action."

He leaned back in his chair and folded his arms, the expression on his face somewhere between amusement and annoyance. "I don't have a Santa suit."

"I'll rent one for you."

"Tucker says you can use the arena and that's all."

"That's fine. It's big enough to freeze for the ice skating and we can do the booths on the other half." She stared back at him, trying to get him to see her vision. "The people who bring their pets here will really like it."

"You know, Layla, and I don't want this to sound rude." He scooted forward again and picked up the map. "But there's nowhere else to take a dog if it gets sick. So...."

"I want to say thank you to my patrons," she said, something storming in her chest she couldn't make sense of. "It's important to me. I—I don't know why, but it is."

Logan's eyes softened and he reached across the table and put one of his hands on hers. "Then it's important to me too." He smiled, and this time it was soft and wonderful and everything Layla wanted in a smile aimed at her.

Her insides turned to pudding, and she ducked her head so Logan couldn't read every emotion currently zipping through her body.

Logan cleared his throat and stood. The absence of his hand on hers left her with a cold pit in her stomach. "Well, I should go." He left her office without looking back, and Layla moved to the doorway to watch him walk down the hall. A sigh escaped her lips and Aria came out of the room next door at the exact right time to hear it.

"Yep," she said. "You've got it bad for him."

"Don't I know it," Layla muttered. She wasn't upset about her growing feelings for Logan. She was worried about how to handle them, what to do about them, and if she could even trust herself to know how she felt.

Logan hadn't acted like he wanted Layla to be, well, less Layla. At least not yet.

CHAPTER
NINE

Logan skipped the elevator in Layla's building. His excitement for their evening together needed to be expended before he knocked on her door. He felt like Rambo, like he needed a good run before he could settle into being himself.

Once on the fifth floor, he took a few seconds to steady his breathing and run his hand through his hair. With his cowboy hat reseated and a grin in place, he walked down the hall to Layla's apartment. She opened the door right when he lifted his hand to knock, and he nearly bashed her in the face.

"Oh." She jumped back at the same time a yelp came from his mouth. "I was just checking to see if you were here."

"I'm here." Logan liked the redness of her lips. Combined with her fair skin and blonde hair, she looked flirty and fun. Sexy.

He swallowed and took in her fall print dress, large splashes of red, gold, and orange all the way down to her ankles. He breathed in the sensual scent of her skin and couldn't stop himself from winding his arms around her and holding her close.

"It's good to see you," he said, his voice hardly his own. He hadn't felt such powerful things for a woman, ever. Half of him wanted to kiss her right now, see if she felt the same things he did. The other half wanted to run in the other direction, take the time to figure out what all these boiling things inside him meant.

"You too," she said, a little breathlessly in his opinion. As he gazed down on her, he realized he didn't need to kiss her to know how she felt about him. It all sat right there in her blue eyes. She definitely liked him too, and Logan loved that the feelings between them seemed to be mutual.

He also detected a slip of fear and that alone kept him from kissing her. He did hold her hand, and open the door for her. He paid for dinner, and the movie, and her popcorn with extra butter. He liked listening to her talk about the animals at the shelter and how she'd looked up the requirements to become a therapy dog trainer.

"You did?" He handed her the tub of popcorn now that she'd settled in her seat.

"Yeah, it's in my office. You should stop by and get it on Monday while you're there."

"Did you look at any of it?" He sat next to her and put his soda in the cup holder between them. "What does it take?"

"You take courses. The best place to do it is Bergin University. I printed some stuff for you about their programs."

Logan could barely swallow the licorice he'd gotten. All it tasted like was wax. What would Darren say if Logan told him he was going to leave Steeple Ridge? Worry gnawed at him. Sam had worked so hard for so long to keep the brothers together, and a pang of sadness sang through Logan. Ben was gone now. Sam too. How would Darren take the news of Logan leaving too?

"Where is Bergin University?" he asked.

"California."

Logan's heart dropped to his boots and rebounded painfully back into its rightful place. "Oh, well that settles that."

Layla looked at him with dozens of questions in her eyes. "What do you mean?"

"I mean I'm not moving all the way across the whole country for a dog training course."

"Why not?"

He shrugged, unwilling to say why. He knew she was a big reason, but they were on date number three, and he didn't want to spook her. Number two, he did have to consider his brother's feelings. He'd talk to Darren about it, probably even Sam. Just because Logan liked to laugh and didn't bother himself with details didn't mean he didn't think through major decisions before making them.

"Logan."

He looked at her, somewhat surprised at the intensity he found in her eyes. "Yeah?"

"Why can't you go to California for the training?"

"I have a job here," he said. "Tucker's not going to let me take off weeks at a time. Darren's here. I have my volunteer work. Who'll take Bones and Ginger Ale over to the kids?" He shrugged and shoved another handful of popcorn in his mouth.

"You should think about it. Things like jobs and brothers can be worked out."

The previews started, and Logan had never been so grateful.

———

THE NEXT EVENING, LAYLA DIDN'T POKE HER HEAD INTO THE hall to check if he was there. He rang the doorbell like a proper gentleman and waited for her to answer. He presented her with the dozen red roses he'd bought on his way over and drew her into his chest. She swayed with him, and he wondered why it had taken him so long to ask her out.

With their date the previous night being successful, he'd promptly accepted her invitation to come by her place for dinner. She'd texted that morning, and Logan had worked quickly to get his chores done in time. As it was, Cody had picked up a few things for him so he could leave early, shower, and get into town.

Though he'd wanted to kiss her goodnight after the movies, she'd ducked her head and slipped her key into the lock on the first try. Logan had dated enough to know the signs that screamed *I'm not ready for you to kiss me!*

He hoped that her invitation to spend time with her in her home would allow her to send a different kind of message.

After a minute of bliss with her in his arms, she stepped out and welcomed him into the apartment. "I hope you like butternut squash."

"As long as it's not made into a pie, squash is fine."

Layla closed the door behind him. "So you don't like Halloween, and you don't like pumpkin pie. Is that it?"

"Pretty much." He drank in the space that screamed Layla. She had dark carpet on the floor and bright white walls. Everything seemed to be in its rightful place, even though she'd clearly been cooking in the kitchen. Logan was beginning to realize how detailed Layla was, how organized, how…everything he wasn't.

"Nice place," he said, running his hand along the back of the couch as he followed her into the kitchen.

"Thanks. These condos are new."

"Where'd you live before this?"

"I rented a little house out on Fourth and Rooster." She shuddered as she lifted a spoon and started stirring the soup. "There were so many spiders out there. Snakes too." She flashed him a smile with her glance. "It's much nicer here."

"I'll bet." He chuckled. "We've got a lot of critters on the farm too."

"Not in the house, I bet."

"No, you're right. Tucker keeps that place fumigated."

"Mm."

"So butternut squash soup, huh?" He looked around and found the frying pan. "With bacon, I see."

"Everything's better with bacon." Layla laughed and Logan joined in. He told her that he'd looked up Bergin University and that their courses were only seven weeks. "So maybe I could do it."

"You should totally do it," she said. "You'd be so good at it, and there's nobody like that here in town. I bet there isn't anybody like that in Burlington either." She ladled soup into bowls, sprinkled bacon on top, and bent to take a sheet pan out of the oven. Bread cut into perfect triangles had been browned to perfection, and she delicately placed two on each bowl at precise angles.

"Wow." Logan whistled. "I didn't know food could look so good."

"We eat with our eyes first," Layla said, leading him to the table. He sat across from her, wondering when his life had turned itself upside down. Everything he'd thought he knew about Layla was all wrong. She was twice as good as he'd imagined. Twice as kind. Twice as beautiful, inside and out. And she could cook.

The talked about the clinic, and Ginger Ale, and her father's job before they moved into her living room with coffee mugs and the promise of chocolate cake later. Logan was thinking about another prize he hoped would come later, and that was kissing Layla.

She snuggled into his side, and they drank coffee to the fake roaring sounds of her electric fireplace. He liked her right beside him, and she seemed to like being there.

When a lull in the conversation presented itself, Logan

finished his coffee and leaned forward to set the mug on the table. He took Layla's from her too, and turned to look at her. "I wanted to ask you something."

Her smile was lazy and soft around the edges. "Yeah?"

"Yeah." He cleared his throat and wished he hadn't drunk so much coffee. It seemed to boil inside of him with an intolerable heat. "We've been out several times, and I, well, I was hoping you…. Wow, this isn't going well."

But he had her attention. Her eyes had sharpened, and she supported her head with her hand, one elbow against the back of the couch. "We've been out several times?" she asked.

He frowned and gave a slight shake of his head. "Yeah. What I'm trying to say is, well, I'm wondering if you'd let me…kiss you…."

She shot to her feet, her eyes panicked now.

"I'll take that as a no." He stood too, a freaky sense of calm descending on him. "It's just that I really like you, and I thought you liked me too."

"I—"

"It's okay. Really." But the way his internal organs twisted said otherwise. At least she couldn't see the agonizing pain he was in. He ducked his head just to make sure his cowboy hat covered his expression. "I'll go."

His hand rested on the doorknob before she said, "Logan, wait."

He turned back to her but didn't look at her. Didn't want her to see the embarrassment and humiliation on his face.

"This has been fun," she started, and Logan knew how this was going to end. And he didn't want to hear it.

"You've said that to me before." His voice sounded like glass in a garbage disposal. "I don't want to hear it again." He twisted the knob and spilled into the hallway. He took several steps down the hall and then came to a full-stop.

He turned around and marched back to Layla's still-open door. "Why are you doing this?" He looked right at her, trying to figure things out, figure *her* out. "I know you like me."

She stood at the end of the couch, a terrified look on her face. "I do like you," ghosted from her lips.

"But you don't want to kiss me." He shoved his hands in his pockets. "That I can actually live with, though I think I'm a pretty good kisser. I mean, no one's ever complained."

"I'm sure they haven't." She hadn't moved or thawed, and every muscle in her body remained tense.

"But I can't figure out why every time I start gettin' close to you, you shut me out." He took a step into her apartment, needing to get a little closer to her. Feel her energy. Try to understand. "Last time, I waited two years before I even allowed myself to look your way again. *Two years*, Layla. I don't want to wait two more years."

"I'm scared."

"Of what?" Logan knew he was big, and broad, and boisterous. She hadn't seemed to mind though. In fact, she seemed to enjoy holding his hand and pressing her cheek to his chest and listening to him laugh.

"Of myself," she said. "I'm scared that once you really know me, you won't like me."

"That's impossible." Logan entered the apartment fully now and closed the door behind him. She was talking, and he wanted to keep it that way. "I know a lot about you. We've spent a lot of time together. I like you just the way you are."

She shook her head. "I just—"

He continued to advance toward her. He took the tips of her fingers into his hand. "You just what?"

He didn't know blue eyes could hold so much terror. But Layla's did when she said, "I have a Three Date Rule, and you're over the limit."

"Three Date Rule?" Logan squinted at her. "What does that mean?"

"It means I only go on three dates with a man. Then it's over."

Logan scoffed, sure she was joking. "That's ridiculous."

Layla's face hardened, and Logan regretted his words. "Sorry," he said quickly. "It's just—why would you have a rule like that for yourself?"

She tugged her fingers away from his. "It doesn't matter why. What matters is that you got three and a half dates, and that means—"

"We're done," he said at the same time as her. An inexplicable wave of anger flowed over him.

"I don't understand you," he said. "And that's okay. Growing up, my mom told me I didn't need to understand women. I just needed to be respectful of them."

"Your mom must've been wonderful."

Logan didn't want Layla's kind words about his mother. He wanted *her*, but she didn't want to give herself to him. To anyone, apparently.

"So I'll respect you. I'm over your limit. I'll go." This time, when he left her apartment, he didn't go back.

CHAPTER
TEN

Layla's phone rang an hour later. She sucked back a sniffle and took a deep breath. "Hello?" she said before answering, hoping her voice didn't sound too nasally. She honestly couldn't tell, so she picked up the call.

"Layla," Rae said. "What is going on with you and Logan?"

Layla rankled at her friend's interference. "Nothing."

"Well, he just left here, and let me tell you, there's something. He is, well, if I didn't know better I'd say he was heartbroken."

"We, well, I made soup for him tonight, and we were talking, and…."

"He told us," Rae said. "You're still doing the three date thing? With *him*?" The way she said *him* wasn't lost on Layla. Like Logan couldn't possibly fall into the same category as other men, and therefore should be exempt from the Three Date Rule.

Of course he should be, she thought, and everything flew into place. "Rae, I have to go."

"What are you going to do?" she practically yelled, as if Layla would still be ale to hear her if she hung up.

"I need to call Logan." She hung up, swiped her keys from the end table, and dialed Logan on her way out the door.

Thankfully, he was a better person than her and answered his phone when she called. Had their positions been reversed, she didn't think she'd have answered if he called.

"Layla," he said instead of hello.

"Where are you?"

"Sitting in my truck."

"Out at Steeple Ridge?" She didn't want him to know Rae had called. Where she'd felt weak and helpless an hour ago, now she felt whole and strong. She started her car.

"No, I'm at the Tonic Barn."

"I'm on my way." She hung up before he could tell her not to come, and she prayed that he'd still be there when she showed up.

She found his truck parked where the white luncheon tent had been a few weeks ago, and she trembled from the cold and from what she needed to do. She managed to walk from her car to his truck and open the passenger door. "Can I get in?"

"Too cold to stay out there," he said, staring straight ahead.

She climbed in and closed the door, sealing the heat inside. "I don't know how much of the story you need," she said. "But I have these Dating Rules to protect myself."

"We've all been hurt in the past," he said. "I get it."

"No, you don't. The rules are for me, but they don't apply to you."

He swung his gaze toward her, and she could drown in the depths of his eyes and die happy. "They don't?"

"I want a fourth date with you." She said the words, and she meant them, but she also knew what a fourth date meant. "And not that this is always true, but I found back when I allowed fourth dates, that *that's* when the first kiss usually happened."

Logan simply stared at her. She hoped the wheels in his mind were turning furiously.

"So I was a date too early, is that it?"

"Only half a date."

"Half a date?" He sighed and turned back to the windshield. "How do two people go on half a date?"

"They double."

He shook his head, a soft chuckle finally popping the awkwardness between them. "So the lunch here at the barn. That didn't count at all."

"We met," she said. "You didn't come pick me up. And you brought your brother. So no, I didn't count it."

He leveled his gaze at her again. "How many dates do I get?"

Layla swallowed—or at least she tried to. Her throat had practically closed on itself. "I don't know."

"I'm gonna be real honest with you Layla. I like you a lot. I wanted to kiss you tonight. Heck, I still do. It makes no sense, because I'm angry with you, but I still want to kiss you." He shook his head again and removed his cowboy hat to wipe his hand through his hair. He settled his gaze on her again and it was pointy and sharp this time.

"I want an unlimited number of dates with you," he said. "I don't want to spook you or freak you out, but I don't keep track of the number of dates I have with a woman. I go by how I feel, and I—" His voice cracked and he took a few seconds to control himself. "I guess I'm requesting that you don't put a number on us. That maybe you can go by how you feel too."

Though it meant blowing her Dating Rules to bits and pieces, Layla nodded. "I like the sound of *us*."

Logan reached for her, and she slid next to him. He lifted her wrist to his lips. "Me too." He twined his fingers with hers and settled their joined hands on his leg. "And I would like to hear the full story of how and why you made up these rules. Someday. Doesn't have to be today."

She laid her head against his bicep, grateful and glad the Lord had given her the strength and clarity of thought to keep Logan in her life. "Thank you," she murmured, and it was for both Logan and the Lord.

———

Layla watched the clock on Monday morning, almost obsessively. Finally, Logan arrived—five minutes before he normally did. He collected Bones's leash and got Ginger Ale out of her kennel. "Hey, Layla," he said in his wonderful cowboy drawl.

She blushed, but ducked her head to let her hair fall down. He scrubbed his hand along Bones's back, the way he always did. He wore that scrumptious white cowboy hat, the way he always did. He grinned at her and made her heart race, the way he always did.

"Didn't see you at church yesterday," he said.

"Wasn't feeling social." Layla gave him a smile that seemed to satisfy him, and he tipped his cowboy hat at her. She hadn't wanted to sit by her friends and gossip about Logan. A slip of humiliation still existed within her that she'd tried to end things with him because he'd exceeded her dating limit.

"I understand that. Going to your fancy salad bar today?"

She laughed, the last remaining bit of tension between them fading away. "Yes, so I'll see you later."

"What about tonight for later?" His fingers traced across the back of her hand. The touch sent shivers and fireworks through her at the same time, an exhilarating sensation that made Layla weak. "The Fall Festival starts today, and they've got the art show at the rec center."

"Sounds fun." Layla had never gotten into the smaller events of the Fall Festival, but if she could wander around a heated building with her hand secured in Logan's, she'd take that over sitting home alone.

"How do you feel about La Ferrovia?"

"I adore La Ferrovia."

"Great, so I'll pick you up at six, and we'll eat and go look at the art." He leaned down and she looked up, and for one horrifying, wonderful moment she thought he'd kiss her right there in the clinic.

He swept his cowboy hat off his head and skated his lips across her cheek. "See you tonight." He turned and walked out, setting his hat back in place and taking the dogs with him.

Layla exhaled and leaned into the counter, completely spent. She stared at the spot he'd last been, wondering if he'd kiss her that night. She really wanted him to kiss her tonight. And to make that happen, she had the distinct feeling she'd have to instigate it. Which meant she needed a plan.

Aria stuck her head in the room. "You ready for lunch? Hazel went to start her car."

"I'm ready." Layla left her paperwork on the counter and stopped by her office for her purse. She managed to wait until the three of them had driven to the country club and gone through the salad bar before she said, "All right, ladies. Logan and I are very near the first kiss stage, and I need help making it happen tonight."

Hazel squealed, dropped her fork, and dug in her purse until she produced a notebook. "Okay, I'll take notes."

Aria laughed, speared another broccoli floret, and jabbed it at Layla. "So he's over the three date threshold. Are the rules out of play?"

Layla stuck a bite of lettuce, cucumber, and bleu cheese in her mouth. She chewed as she shrugged one shoulder. Swallowed, and said, "There are no rules when one is dating Logan Buttars."

Hazel scrawled DATING across the top of the paper and beamed at it. And for the first time in ten years, Layla felt the same level of joy at the prospect of truly dating a man.

"You don't think he'll kiss you?" Aria asked.

Layla didn't want to tell them how stupid she'd been, but she took a deep breath and started on the story anyway. She finished with, "So I think I'll have to be the one to kiss him." She glanced at Hazel and Aria. They were both nearly finished eating, but she'd hardly taken a bite. "Tell me what to do. It's been a long time for me."

She ate as they gave her ideas, gushed over the fact that Layla had broken her rules, and discussed the best places in town for a first kiss.

"Wait. He can't just kiss me at the door?" Fear took hold of Layla's heart. "Like, when the date is over, and I can hurry inside?"

"Why would you want to hurry inside afterward?" Aria looked truly perplexed. She shook her head, the determination on her face obvious. "No, you kiss him early in the date. Then you get to kiss him *again* when it's over."

Layla had been out of the dating game for far too long. "Oh, all right. So we're going to La Ferrovia and then the rec center. It's supposed to rain tonight. I don't think we'll be wandering around town or anything."

"Take an umbrella," Hazel suggested. "Then you can

walk around town, and an evening kiss, in the rain, under an umbrella—so romantic." She actually sighed before jotting down the idea.

"How do I kiss him?" Layla pushed her mostly eaten salad away. "I mean, just stop on the sidewalk and be like —?" Her mind blanked.

"You're thinking too hard about this," Aria said. "Just let it happen. You'll know."

Layla nodded, but her nerves still rioted. She did not know. She hadn't kissed anyone since Rick, and their first kiss had happened almost eleven years ago.

CHAPTER
ELEVEN

"Wait," Logan commanded Bones, who obeyed immediately. Ginger took another step before pausing, much better than she normally did. He'd arrived before the recess bell had rung, something he tried to do so he could condition Ginger to the noise, the activity, the rush of students who came in at that time.

She'd been getting better and better at holding still, right at his side, and just watching the kids as they flowed past. Bones laid down, his tongue out of his mouth because wow, the elementary school administration really kept their building warm when it was cold outside.

The bell rang, and Bones closed his eyes. Ginger's ears went up, but she didn't try to cower behind him the way she had in the past.

"Lay down," he said. Ginger didn't move. "Ginger," he tried again, glad when she looked at him. "Lay down." He gave her the hand signal, and she reluctantly settled onto the floor just as the first teacher brought his class down the hall. "Stay."

Logan and his two dogs waited until the halls had quieted, and both Bones and Ginger Ale performed spectacularly. "Good job, Ginger." The German shepherd jumped to her feet and he treated her with a piece of liver from his pocket.

"All right, guys. Let's work." He took them down the hall to the special education classroom, where they'd be greeted by six kids ranging in age from eight to twelve. Two of them were in wheelchairs, and the other four had been taught to let the dogs come to them.

Logan entered the room and immediately unleashed Bones. The white lab wandered over to Louisa, his favorite little girl. She rubbed under his jaw and grinned at him. "Bones," she said, apparently one of the only words she ever spoke.

She looked up for Ginger Ale and reached one hand out to the dog.

Logan kept Ginger right at his side as he took her over to Louisa. "Ginger Ale," Logan said in a clear voice. "Sit."

The dog sat and Louisa gave her a pat.

"Stay," Logan told Ginger and he thumped Bones on the shoulder. "Go on."

Bones left Louisa to Ginger Ale and made his way through the group of special needs kids. They patted him. Logan gave Brian, a boy with Down Syndrome, a handful of liver treats and said he could have Bones do some tricks.

Brian led Bones through shaking, sitting, lying down, and giving high five. "What else can he do, Mister Logan?"

"Let's try touch," Logan said, looking Brian right in the eye. "You use two fingers, like this." He held up his first two fingers, right together. "Bones has to touch them with his nose. Not his mouth. Nose." He touched his fingers to his own nose. "Three times before he gets a treat. Like this."

He held his two fingers out to his side and said, "Touch."

Bones swung around and nosed his fingers. Logan switched them to the other side. "Touch." Bones nosed him again. Logan held his fingers up near his chest, which would require Bones to jump a bit. "Touch."

Bones complied, and all the kids watching started talking, and cheering, and laughing. Logan grinned at them. "He's pretty smart, right? Like you guys." He gave Bones a piece of liver and looked at Brian. "Okay, bud. Your turn."

Brian held his two fingers out to his side. "Touch," he said in his thick voice. Bones turned toward him, but didn't move. "Touch," Brian repeated.

Bones touched his nose to Brian's fingers, who sent a hearty laugh around the room. He gave Bones a piece of liver before Logan could say, "Remember he has to do three touches to get a treat."

"Oh, sorry, Mister Logan."

"No problem. Try it again." Logan adored Brian, who always hugged him and both dogs before they could leave. He liked watching Louisa stroke Ginger Ale. He loved that these two simple animals could bring so much joy to these kids.

As he continued working, moving the dogs from child to child, he knew he needed to do more with his life than he was currently doing. He was young still. Bergin University had certificate programs that only took weeks. He needed to look into their degrees as well.

A feeling flowed over him, and he recognized the whispers of the Lord, guiding him and directing him toward a different future.

After he'd finished with the kids and gotten his hugs, he took the dogs out to the truck. It had started to rain a little, and he focused on the droplets of water on the windshield as he dialed Darren.

"What's up?" his brother answered. His breathing sounded labored, as if he was shoveling out horse stalls—which he probably was.

"Darren, I'm thinking about going to college," Logan said.

Everything between them seemed to pause, even though they weren't in the same physical space. "College. Huh." Darren didn't even make his tone questioning, almost like he'd already known Logan wasn't content at Steeple Ridge. And that wasn't even true. He loved Steeple Ridge. Loved Island Park. There was just more out there, and Logan felt like now was the time to find it.

"I want to be a therapy dog trainer," Logan said. "Or something like that. I love horses too, but I think I would really excel at assisting people through canine therapy."

"You'd be really good at that."

"That's what Layla said." Logan smiled just thinking about her. In the same breath, his hopes of going to college plummeted. Her life was here in Island Park, and Vermont was about as far from California as one could get and still be in the same country.

"You should look into it," Darren said, like he knew Logan had barely glanced at the university's website. "I can help you tonight if you want."

"I'm going out with Layla tonight."

"Tomorrow then."

"Tomorrow," Logan confirmed, and he hoped Darren wouldn't feel too abandoned if Logan went off to college and left him at Steeple Ridge all alone.

———

LOGAN WAS LATE, AND HE HATED BEING LATE MORE THAN anything. He voice texted Layla that he was on his way about five minutes before he was supposed to arrive. With her parking situation, he'd need to be pulling in now, and he was barely to the outskirts of town.

I'll meet you out front, she texted. The light where Logan waited turned green, so he didn't respond. Ten minutes later—why did she have to live on the other side of downtown?—he pulled into the circular drive in front of her building to find her perched on a bench.

She wore a pair of dark blue jeans and a sweater the color of Dijon mustard. She stood when he came to a stop and he leapt from the truck to help her up. She laughed as he swept his hand around her waist, and he couldn't help joining in.

"Sorry I'm late. We had a miscommunication about the hot water."

"Oh?"

"Darren has a date with Farrah tonight too."

"And we're not doubling?"

"I didn't want to deal with those pesky half-dates." He gave her a quick smirk, and her eyes widened. He chuckled and opened the passenger door. "I'm joking, Layla. Let's go eat."

He enjoyed dinner immensely, and not only because La Ferrovia served those spicy sausages he liked with his pasta carbonara. The conversation flowed easily, the way it had before he'd learned of her Three Date Rule. She was flirty, and fun, and finally everything he'd been looking for in a woman.

He liked that she ate when she went out with him. That she asked him questions about his work, his family, his hopes and dreams.

"I'm going to look into the degree programs at Bergin University," he said.

She took a moment to absorb the news by lifting her soda glass to her lips. "How long do those take?"

"Years." He watched her, but she didn't flinch or swallow or anything. "I wouldn't start right away," he said. "I mean, it's almost October already, and surely those programs start in the fall."

Layla leaned back in her chair and regarded him with

eyes harboring a secret. "You haven't looked at them, have you?"

"I glanced through their degree programs," he said evasively. She didn't need to know it had taken him thirty seconds to read the descriptions. While Logan wasn't exactly detail-oriented when it came to planning things, he'd been surviving somehow.

"I looked." She gave him a teensy smile that made his blood run hotter. "Want me to tell you about them?"

"I'm capable of looking things up."

"You just don't like it."

"You do?"

"Sure," she said. "I like making plans. Remember that map of the winter carnival?"

Logan remembered, and he released his defenses. She wasn't making fun of him and his lack of organization. She actually liked learning all the details. "So tell me."

"All right, so there's a two-year program where you can earn an Associate's Degree in Assistance Dog Education. I think that's what you should do. You train dogs and place them with people with specific disabilities."

"That sounds like what I'd like."

"The Bachelor's Degree is more about studying dogs and their relationship with humans. I think you want to work more in the therapy arena, so the Associate's program is enough."

"Two years." Logan glanced up when the waiter arrived.

"Dessert tonight?" he asked.

"Yeah," Logan said, accepting the menu. "But we'll

want it to go. Let's see." He pretended to study the menu though he knew exactly what he wanted. "I'll take the tuxedo cheesecake. And she'll have…." He glanced at her.

She watched him with pure amusement in her eyes. "Go on then. You think you're so smart."

Logan swallowed, the pressure of ordering for her nearly choking him. Then his eyes landed on exactly what she'd like. "Apple pie crisp. Can we get the ice cream on the side?"

"I have ice cream at home," she said. "We can't carry it around the art show."

"Oh, right." He slapped the dessert menu closed and handed it back to the waiter, who smiled as he walked away.

"How'd I do?"

"Decently well."

"Tell me you haven't ordered that before."

She said nothing, which made Logan laugh. "I knew I nailed it."

"Arrogant about it too."

Logan sobered. "Not arrogant. Just glad I got you something you'll like."

Layla gave him that smile again, the one that made him want to lunge across the table and take her face in his hands and kiss her. "It's the only thing I've ordered here," she said. "I love it."

"You like traditional things," he said. "That's how I knew."

"I like traditional things?"

"Sure. Pumpkin pie. Old barns. Sleigh rides."

"And that translates to apple pie for dessert?"

"It's an American classic." Logan gave the waiter his credit card and a few minutes later, they carried a bag with their desserts out into the falling rain.

"Oh, I was gonna walk, but—"

"I brought an umbrella." Layla produced one from seemingly nowhere and opened it above them. She tucked her hand in his elbow and said, "We have time to walk, don't we?"

"Sure."

But she didn't lead him a couple of blocks east to the rec center. Instead, she went down Main Street, where a large sidewalk decorated both sides of the street and made a walkway in the middle too.

"I came to Island Park only five years ago," Layla said. "I was only supposed to stay a year."

"Why'd you stay longer then?"

"I fell in love with the town," she said. Logan liked the happy lilt in her voice. Liked that she'd followed her heart and stayed here, even if it wasn't in her plan. Wondered if she'd come to California with him if he asked her to.

Better kiss her first, he thought. After all, Sam had taught him that a woman wasn't your girlfriend until that first kiss.

Logan's resolve tightened. He wasn't going to kiss Layla tonight. Maybe not for a while. He didn't want to scare her off, and they'd been getting along so great since he'd practically proclaimed his undying interest in her a few nights ago. Since she'd given up her dating rules. He wasn't going to make her regret doing that for him.

No, if there was any kissing to be done, she'd have to get that ball rolling. Logan didn't think she would, so he kept her on his arm and asked her questions about her family vacations growing up.

They rounded the corner and went down by the post office and back up the street, past the library. She led him in front of the clinic and though the rec center sat right there in front of them at the end of the block, Layla turned and took him into a park he hadn't visited before.

Small lamps lit the walkway, and Logan felt as if he'd stepped from the real world into a magical one. "What's the name of this park?" he asked.

"Peacock Park."

"Why is everything named after birds here?"

"I'm not sure." Layla pointed to her right. "But I know why this park is Peacock. There's a little refuge for them here."

Several seconds passed before Logan could make out the shapes of the birds hunkered under the trees. "Oh, I see them. They live here?" He swung his attention to her for a brief moment.

"All year round."

The rain continued to ping against her umbrella as they walked. She fell silent, and Logan detected a definite hint of nervousness from her. "Do you like art?" he asked. "Because we don't have to go to the show. We could—"

"I don't want to go to the show," she said. "But I like art just fine."

His step faltered. "So you like art, but you don't want to go to the show." Logan liked simple. Dinner and a movie. Lunch and a tribute to an old barn. He'd never planned elaborate dates. Didn't even know how.

"What did you have in mind?" He turned toward her, and the light from the lamp a few feet away caught in her eyes. Without thinking and without waiting for her to answer his question, he reached up and swept a lock of her hair off her face. "You're so pretty," he whispered.

She looked like she'd eaten something bad for dinner. Her skin seemed way too far on the gray side, and Logan almost suggested he take her home when she said, "Can I kiss you?"

He didn't know how to answer. "No one's ever asked me that before."

"I'm asking you."

He stepped closer to her and removed his cowboy hat so it wouldn't land on the soaking wet ground in a silent *yes, please kiss me.*

She stretched up on her toes and Logan put both arms around her, holding her tight. He closed his eyes, took in a deep breath of her distinctly feminine scent, and tried to calm the thundering of his heart.

Finally, finally, her lips touched his, and everything in Logan sparked. Her fingers trailed along his neck and into his hair. A groan started somewhere deep in his gut, and he deepened the kiss, hoping it would never end.

CHAPTER
TWELVE

ayla had no idea kissing a man could be so wonderful. She'd forgotten the thrill of a strong touch along her back. Forgotten the rush of adrenaline when mouths touched. Forgotten everything that was good about this human connection.

And Logan hadn't lied. He was a very good kisser. Very good indeed.

He eventually broke the connection between them, tucking her against his chest. His pulse bounced around like a ping pong ball, a fact which made Layla smile against the fabric of his jacket. Her own heart rippled like a flag in a stiff breeze, but at least she knew the feelings between them ran both ways.

"Layla," he whispered in that same sexy, throaty way he'd spoken when he'd said she was pretty. Hazel had suggested Peacock Park for their first kiss, but neither of her friends had given her a concrete idea for how to do it.

Logan had asked on Saturday, and Layla thought that tactic was as good as any.

"Hmm?"

He pulled away from her but didn't say anything else. He simply kissed her again.

Everything Aria had taught her came true. She didn't want to slip behind a closed door after their first kiss. Because this second one was so much better. So was the one she gave him once they'd made it through the park and back to his truck. And when he pressed her into her closed apartment door and kissed her so completely she thought she'd fall if not for his strong arms holding her in place, she didn't think she'd ever want to kiss another man.

———

"I can't believe you don't want to dress up." Layla took a bite of the salad Logan had brought her from the bread company. They'd take any of their sandwiches and make it into a salad, and he'd quickly learned she liked bleu cheese more than ranch, turkey more than ham, and never, ever tomatoes.

"I dress up everyday." He gave her a wolfish grin and took another bite of his California club sandwich, complete with sprouts and avocado.

Layla giggled but she detected something underneath his joke. "Have you applied to Bergin yet?"

"No, Darren and I are still talking."

"About what?"

"I'm…I'm just making sure he's okay with things."

"What kind of things?" Layla peered at him so she wouldn't miss a single expression on his face.

"Twin things." Logan put his sandwich down and brushed the crumbs from his fingers. "I know it's dumb, and I know he wants me to be happy, but we literally have never lived apart. We share the same room now, even though there's enough rooms for us to have our own."

He shrugged like it was no big deal, but Layla had been on at least eight more dates with Logan—she'd actually stopped counting—and she sensed something lurking just beyond his eyes. They didn't hold as much life as they usually did, and though he was still his jovial, carefree self, a more serious edge lurked within him too.

Worry wormed through her on his behalf, and she reached across the table and curled her fingers around his. "Well, let me know what I can do to help."

The life she was used to blazed in his eyes, and he said, "He's still seeing Farrah, so that's good."

"Yeah?"

"Yeah, she's the first one he's dated since we moved here."

"Yeah, you Buttars brothers didn't get off that farm much. Good thing Ben branched out so the rest of you could see you'd be okay without each other." Layla regretted the words as soon as she said them. "I mean, I'm sorry Logan. That came out wrong."

He shook his head like it was no big deal. "It's fine." But he didn't pick up his sandwich to finish it.

"I know you guys really relied on each other after your

parents died. I didn't mean—" She clamped her mouth shut, because she didn't know what she didn't mean. "It was a joke."

"I know." Logan gazed at her evenly. "I have to go." He plucked his chips from her desk and leaned over to kiss her. "Call you later." He didn't seem upset, but the tenderness in his touch was absent, and he didn't look back and wave to her the way he'd taken to doing the last few weeks.

When he called that night, she asked, "So are we really not going to the Halloween party?"

He sighed, one giant heave of breath. "What are you dressing up as?"

"I haven't decided yet."

"It's next weekend. If the queen of Halloween hasn't decided, what does that mean for the rest of us?"

"Ha ha." Layla rolled her eyes though no one but Sweet Pea was there to see her. She patted the dog on the head and picked up the wooden spoon to stir her chicken and wild rice soup. This wasn't a new recipe, but one of her mother's she'd grown up loving. Layla had added another chicken bouillon cube somewhere over the years, as well as a dash of hot sauce right on top of the broth before she ate it. She also grilled her chicken before adding it, while her mother boiled it.

"What's the soup of the day?" Logan asked.

She told him, and then asked if she could bring Sweet Pea out to Steeple Ridge that weekend.

"You just want to poke around the arena and add to your map."

"I do not," Layla said. "Okay, maybe a little. But I want to see you too, and poor Sweet Pea hasn't been out of the apartment in a few days."

"You want to see me too. How flattering."

"Logan," she practically whined.

He laughed, the sound almost as delicious as the soup simmering on the stove. "I'll see you Thursday, Lay." He hung up before she could fully process that he'd just given her a nickname.

She didn't mind it terribly, but what could she call him. Log?

She laughed out loud for herself and ladled up a bowl of soup.

Thursday came, and Layla saw Logan for a few minutes before he took the dogs over to the elementary school for their therapy. "Saw" wasn't quite the right word. "Kissed" would've fit better. She liked this still new and exhilarating relationship where she could kiss him right in the clinic, on the sidewalk, in his truck, in her apartment.

Though it had been a few weeks since their first kiss in Peacock Park, Layla still felt like every aspect of their relationship was shiny and bright. Logan's infectious optimism and quick smile had something to do with that, and Layla cherished every moment she spent with him.

The promise of him leaving Island Park hung over their heads, but they hadn't spoken of it again. She wasn't sure what Logan had decided, if he'd decided anything at all.

Layla hadn't had much time to think about it anyway. She'd been too busy organizing the clinic Halloween party, and getting things lined up for the winter carnival. She'd assigned the ice skating to Hazel, the reindeer ring toss to Aria, the elf pond to Jack, another colleague who managed all her vaccination orders.

With Logan running the sleigh, Layla was free to run the hot chocolate and doughnut table. Missy and Tucker had agreed to stack hay bales and make a bit of a maze for the younger kids, and Darren had even agreed to section off part of the arena for the pets.

Layla had a call out to Mike at the grocery store to see if they'd donate the doughnuts and hot chocolate, but she was prepared to purchase them if not. She checked the plans every morning when she arrived at work, in the quiet minutes before anyone else showed up.

The alarm on her phone sounded and she pulled herself from her charts. She shrugged into her coat and shouldered her purse. "I'm going to meet Logan for lunch," she told Hazel as she passed the reception desk.

"Have fun." Hazel grinned at her and picked up the phone as it rang.

She almost ran straight into Logan as she went out the front door. "Oh, hey. I thought we were meeting at the waffle house."

He took his hand in hers and turned back the way he'd come. "I have something to show you." He didn't look or sound happy, and Layla took quick tiny steps to keep up with him, a rush of anxiety infecting her.

"What is it?"

He opened the door for her and helped her up. "They've divided the Tonic Barn land and they're selling it." His eyes glittered dangerously and he slammed the door before walking around the front of the truck.

He climbed in. "Darren said Farrah told him about it last night. I drove by on my way here, and there's a huge sign out front."

Layla's mind whirred. "They're going to build on the Tonic Barn land?"

"Yes." He passed Pheasant Drive and Crow's Crescent before adding, "I hope they're going to keep the barn."

"I'm sure they are. Why else would they have had that ceremony?"

He cut her a dark look. "Maybe it was a good-bye ceremony."

Layla started shaking her head. "No. No, the Sellers wouldn't allow it."

"They don't own it anymore."

"The Olsen's wouldn't allow it either. They live on the land. Surely they're going to preserve the barn."

Logan turned into the dirt lot and bumped toward the huge sign that loitered at the end of the road. It seemed so out of place. Though the wind seemed to have a personal vendetta against Island Park today, Logan put the truck in park and leapt from it. Layla joined him and together, they studied the sign.

"See? They're keeping the barn." Layla pointed, though the spot where the barn would remain was much too high for her to reach.

"I see it." Logan tucked his hands into his jacket pockets and remained stoic. "I still...I don't know. It just seems wrong to parcel this farmland and sell it."

She nudged him with her shoulder. "Maybe you should buy a lot. Build yourself a house where you can train all your dogs and take them all over the northeast, matching them to people who are going to benefit from them."

He wrapped his arm around her shoulders and tucked her into his body. "You should buy a lot. Build a small house with a big yard for Sweet Pea. Since you don't like to clean, that should work."

"You forget how much I dislike yard work."

"I did forget that." He pressed his lips to her forehead. "Come on, let's go get some waffles."

CHAPTER
THIRTEEN

Logan hated everything about Halloween. He disliked pumpkins on a fundamental level. He couldn't understand why anyone would wear the color orange, let alone decorate with it. And all those scary witches, ghosts, and werewolves? No.

Layla had decided to dress up as Minnie Mouse, and she'd very politely—and with a gallon of teasing twinkles in her eyes—asked him to "pretty please wear a pair of Mickey Mouse ears."

Which meant he could *not* wear his cowboy hat. She'd given the hideous ears to him on Monday when he'd gone to the clinic to get the dogs. And he'd told her he'd go with her to the church's Halloween chili cook-off. It was in two hours, and he couldn't back out now.

He worked through sunset, pushing his muscles to their breaking point, so he could focus on the pain instead of on how ridiculous he would look in pair of Disney ears.

He couldn't remember the last time he hadn't worn his hat. He wore it everywhere, all the time. It was the first thing he put on in the morning and the last thing he took off at night.

He wondered if he could position the ears over his hat in any way. Frustrated he was still thinking about it, he dug in his shovel and scooped out another load of straw and manure. Dig and lift. He moved horses from one stall to another. Fed them. Swept the barn. He worked until he was going to be late, and for maybe the first time, he didn't care.

"You're not goin' to the church party?" Darren leaned in the doorway of the barn, his arms folded, showered and cologned up, and wearing all his best cowboy clothes. A flash of irritation mixed with jealousy with a force so strong, Logan scowled.

"I'm going."

"You're gonna be late."

I don't care, Logan thought, but instead he leaned his shovel against the wall and stormed past his brother, who chuckled like he knew exactly why Logan was so upset.

Twenty minutes later, Logan tossed the Mickey Mouse ears on the bench seat of the truck, glad Darren had gotten a ride into town with Tucker. Logan would wear the stupid ears for thirty seconds to appease Layla. But no way he was eating dinner and playing games with those silly ears on.

He called Layla when he hit the highway, and she answered with, "Hey, where are you?"

"I'm sorry," he said. "I'm running late, and I just left."

"It's okay. They haven't started yet."

Logan felt like he'd swallowed a brick, and he hadn't even gotten to the party yet. "You know, I've secretly been hoping it would be over by the time I got there."

"You're not joking."

"Not even a little bit."

Silence poured through the line, and Logan regretted his statement. "Layla, I'm sorry. I just—"

"Hate Halloween," they said together.

The background noise disappeared, and Layla said, "I'll meet you out front and we'll go to the country club. They're having prime rib tonight."

"Layla, that's not—"

"I don't want you to be miserable. It's fine."

Logan didn't know what to say. He really didn't want to go to the party, but it was everything Layla lived for.

"We can go for a half an hour," he said. "How about that?"

"I don't want you to be unhappy."

"If we don't go, *you'll* be unhappy."

"Thirty minutes, huh?"

"Thirty minutes." Logan glanced at the ears. "And I don't think I can wear the ears. I'm sorry."

Layla trilled out a laugh. "Logan, I didn't think for a single second you'd wear those ears."

He released his tension and exhaled. "All right, Layla. Let's get this over with."

Layla waited on the curb on Rooster Avenue, her pink and white spotted Minnie dress blowing in the wind.

Logan grinned at her as he pulled into the parking lot and found a space. She met him at his door.

"Will you put the ears on for me?" She batted her over-sized eyelashes at him. "Maybe we can just take a picture of the two of us before we go in."

Logan thought he might do anything for Layla, so he took off his cowboy hat and reached for the Mickey Mouse ears. He put them on and said, "So? How do I look?"

"So handsome." She crowded right into his side and pressed her cheek to his. Holding out her phone, she clicked a picture of the two of them and peered at it. "Aw, we are so cute." She turned the phone so he could see it, and he had to admit that he liked seeing her so close to him, both of their smiles radiating genuine happiness.

His phone dinged as he took off the ears.

"Now you have it t-too," she said, her teeth chattering.

Logan swept his cowboy hat back onto his head and Layla into his arms. "Let's go inside where it's warm."

She pressed closer to his chest and tipped her head back, a beautiful smile on her face. Logan kissed her, the fire between them instant and almost enough to ward off the near-winter chill.

They went inside together, and it looked like a piñata had thrown up. So many colors, so many textures, so many voices talking. Though Logan usually liked parties and celebrations, this one felt out of his league.

Several women who'd flirted with him and his brothers when they'd first arrived in Island Park eyed him and Layla. He spotted Ben—dressed as a police officer—and Rae—dressed as a criminal—and went in their direction.

"You came." Ben blinked at him in surprise.

"We're only here for thirty minutes," Layla said.

"So you're not going to eat?" Rae slid into the chair next to Ben. "Pastor Gray makes his famous red bean chili every year. It's never lost." She took a bite and moaned. "It's this perfect blend of textures and spices and heat. And —" She stabbed her spoon toward the buffet line. "Phil Madsen brought the cornbread. It has real corn kernels in it." She slathered a healthy amount of butter on her cornbread and stuck a piece in her mouth.

"We could eat here," Logan said. "I don't care about going to the country club."

Layla searched his face, and he chuckled. "Really, Layla." He leaned closer, his lips practically catching on her earlobe as he said, "Without the ears, I'm fine."

"The ears are sexy," she whispered back with a giggle, and Ben cleared his throat. He gave Logan a look that said, *You're not alone, bro,* and embarrassment heated Logan's face. He stepped back and joined his hand with Layla's.

They got in line, and Logan asked, "Are you a spicy chili eater? Or more mild?"

"What do you think?"

"Mild." He picked up a paper bowl that seemed much too small for peppers, and onions, and beans.

"You didn't even have to think about it."

"You like butternut squash soup," he said.

"I add hot sauce to my mother's chicken and wild rice soup, I'll have you know."

"Why haven't I had that one?"

Layla lifted one shoulder in a shrug and dished herself

some of Pastor Gray's chili. Logan copied her and took two pieces of cornbread and a little plastic container of honey butter. He returned to the table with Ben and Rae, glad when Tucker and Missy joined them—sans costume.

"You guys don't dress up either?" Logan stared at their perfectly normal clothes. Something shiny distracted him, and he glanced in the direction of a man dressed in aluminum foil and wearing a metal funnel on his head. "Unbelievable."

Layla turned in the Tin Man's direction too, a small gasp leaving her lips. Maybe from the shimmery silver paint covering every inch of exposed skin on the man's body. "He's totally going to win the costume contest."

"He's going to win a trip to the emergency room," Logan muttered. "That's exterior paint, not body paint, and it's full of chemicals."

Tucker shook his head and said, "I hate Halloween," and Logan felt in him a kindred spirit.

———

A WEEK LATER, LAYLA CURLED INTO LOGAN'S SIDE ON THE couch in his living room. She didn't come out to Steeple Ridge very often, but she fit when she did. She'd looked at the arena again, made him take the same measurements he'd taken a few weeks ago, and proclaimed it too cold to do much more.

He'd put milk on to boil for hot chocolate, and Sweet Pea and Rambo were frolicking in the frost-covered grass in the front yard.

"Who's older?" Layla asked.

"Hmm?" Logan kept his eyes closed, the exhaustion that always overcame him with the season change ever-present now that the sun rose so late and set so soon.

"You or Darren?"

"What do you think?" This had become their favorite game, and Logan liked the easy banter between them as they tried to guess things about each other. He felt like he knew her pretty well, what from observing her for two years before finally asking her out.

"Darren."

"What gave it away?"

"He seems…more mature."

Logan's eyes popped open. "More mature? You don't think I'm mature?"

She twisted and lifted herself so her face was even with his. A playful smile danced across her face. "You're practically perfect in every way."

"So now I'm a woman?" Logan shook his head. "This isn't going well."

Layla giggled and kissed him, something different in her touch. He liked the urgency of her movement, the passion she always poured into everything she did.

She broke their kiss. "I wanted to ask you to come home with me for Thanksgiving," she whispered, her forehead pressed against his and her eyes still closed.

Surprise and fear shot through Logan. He didn't know what to say, and his brain wasn't allowing thoughts to align. He couldn't wait too long, so he blurted, "Do I have to eat pumpkin pie?"

She opened her eyes and shook her head, her gaze intense and slightly worried.

Logan said, "Sure, Thanksgiving."

Layla grinned, stroked her fingers down the side of his face in a way that felt very loving, and kissed him again.

Logan wasn't sure, because he'd never been in love before, but as he kissed Layla he sure felt himself falling, and falling fast.

At the same time, *Thanksgiving* screamed in the back of his mind. Just like he'd never fallen in love, he'd never dated anyone seriously enough to go home to meet their family. As their kiss ended and she settled against his chest again, he was sure he'd never live up to Layla's proclamation of *practically perfect in every way*.

CHAPTER
FOURTEEN

Layla tried half a dozen pumpkin pie recipes—including a pumpkin chiffon that was seven shades of wrong—before she gave up trying to convince Logan the holiday dessert was delicious. Even she didn't want to eat another piece for a while. And Meredith and Danny, her next-door neighbors who usually loved her leftovers, had actually requested she not bring them any more pie.

But her parents adored pumpkin pie, and she worried over every little detail. From who would drive to Boston, to where Logan would sleep in their tiny downtown apartment, to how her sisters would act.

She clicked on her laptop and attached the acceptable conversation topics she'd come up with that week. She'd warned Logan that Vanessa and Alice could be… interesting.

"He grew up with three brothers," Layla muttered to

herself as she sent the email. Last week, she'd asked everyone to please avoid the topic of Halloween, and she'd received dozens of texts of old pictures of her dressed up for the holiday.

Logan didn't seem as concerned about visiting her family as Layla did. Typical. Nothing really seemed to ruffle Logan's feathers. She had her folder of plans at-the-ready anyway, and the event was still two weeks away.

I'm here, he texted, and Layla leapt to her feet. They were going to a rendition of Shrek the Musical at the high school that evening, but she didn't think he was coming for another forty-five minutes.

I know I'm early, but I wanted to show you something. Can you come down now?

"Give me ten minutes," Layla dictated into her phone as she hurried into her bedroom to change out of her work clothes. She'd let herself get distracted by Thanksgiving again, and for the millionth time, she wondered why she'd invited him if it was going to prevent her from sleeping.

She sent the message as she searched for her deep purple corduroy pants. They went with everything, like jeans, but still made her feel like she'd dressed up. She paired it with a gray short-sleeved sweater with a cable print on the front and slipped into a pair of black ankle boots. Without time to do much with her hair, she scrubbed her fingers through it and called it good. And extra slick of lip gloss later, and she hit the elevator button.

Logan waited in the circle drive, his truck running. Mother Nature had certainly decided winter should come early, something both Layla and Logan disliked. She'd joked that they finally had some common ground, but he'd been real serious when he'd said, "I think we have a lot in common, Lay. You don't think we get along?"

Of course she thought they got along, and he had never once mentioned how intense she was, or how her details drove him nuts. But somewhere deep down inside her, Layla was waiting for it to happen.

"Hey." She scooted all the way across the seat and dropped a kiss on his cheek. "What's going on?"

"You're wearin' good shoes?" He checked out her feet. "Good enough. Let's go."

"Good enough for what?"

"I bought something."

Layla's eyebrows shot up. "You bought something I have to be wearing good shoes to see? Oh, I can't wait."

She didn't have to wait long. Logan drove south for a few blocks and flipped around to park on the street adjacent to the Olsen farm and the Tonic Barn. He killed the engine and got out, reaching back for her. He didn't let go of her hand as the walked.

"So my parents left each of us boys an inheritance. Mine's just been sittin' around for twelve years, because I had no idea what to do with it. I still don't." He gazed into the night sky, but the storm clouds obscured any stars.

Layla hadn't heard him speak much of his parents or how they died. He hadn't said anything about the programs at Bergin in a long time either. She was slowly learning that just because Logan had a quick smile and was one of the best kissers on the planet didn't mean he didn't think deeply about things.

"I feel a bit lost," he continued, the crunch of their steps over the frosted gravel loud in the darkness surrounding them. "But I know one thing. Two things, actually. One, I want to be a service dog trainer. Darren is helping me get what I need to apply for the Associate's program at Bergin."

Her breath steamed in the air in front of her as her heart shriveled down by one size. "Bergin University is in California."

"It sure is." His grip on her hand didn't loosen.

"What's the second thing you're sure of?" Layla didn't want it to revolve around her, yet at the same time, she really did. She longed to hear him proclaim how much he cared about her, and her pulse pounded out several extra beats in rapid succession.

"I want to live in Island Park," Logan said, sending simultaneous relief and disappointment through Layla.

"So I'm going to go to school in California for a couple of years, and then I'm going to come back here and build my life." He stopped walking, way down on the opposite end of the barn.

He nodded toward the empty land. "Right here. I bought this lot."

Layla turned to survey it, but it was dark, and all the land looked the same. Like a field.

"I wasn't sure if I should buy next to the barn or far from it. I figured there'd still be a lot of tourists, and all that repainting, and well, this lot is one of the bigger ones and the dogs will like that."

She spun toward him, hardly daring to hope too much. "Dogs? Plural?"

Logan gazed at her, all sense of his usual joviality completely gone. "I'm workin' on being sure of a third thing." He reached up with his free hand and pushed her hair off her face. His expression radiated fondness, and if Layla was willing to admit it—love.

"Oh yeah?"

"Maybe someday." His voice caught and he cleared his throat. "Maybe someday, I'd have a wife, and maybe she'd have a dog, you know? So the yard needs to be big enough for plural dogs."

He hadn't come right out and said anything. But the way he looked at her, and the way he kissed her in the next moment, and Layla could imagine the words for herself.

And so, the next day in the quiet half hour before anyone else came into the clinic, Layla started a new planner. One she'd dreamt of for as long as she could remember. One she'd put on a shelf in the very back of her life for a decade. One she was ready to dust off and open again, this time with Logan's name on the front.

A wedding planner.

She let herself sketch what the reception would look like. Her wedding would not be in a Sports Complex, oh no. Even though Rae had made the space intimate and romantic with trellises and plants, Layla didn't want an outdoor wedding.

She sketched the church, with it's sloping floors toward the front and the wide, sweeping stained glass window on the south wall.

She put herself in a strapless gown that trailed behind her for what felt like miles. Every step would require a powerful leg muscle to fire, and she added *Start working out* to her list. After all, she wanted to be able to walk toward her groom.

A click sounded somewhere outside her wedding fantasy, and Layla threw her pen into a drawer. She'd barley put the notebook—not a fancy planner at all—in her bottom filing cabinet drawer when Hazel said, "Morning."

"Morning." Layla didn't turn, but stayed focused on the filing drawer until it locked. With her heart bobbing against the roof of her mouth, she finally twisted toward the door.

"How was the play last night?" Hazel leafed through the clinic mail, the wedding planner nowhere near her mind.

"Just great for a high school play."

"Were the mics loud enough?"

"For once, yes." Layla shrugged into her lab coat and sat at her desk, scanning for any evidence of her wedding plans. She pulled the folder containing her drawings, lists, and contracts for the winter carnival toward her.

Hazel finally tossed the pile on Layla's desk. Her eyes landed on the folder. "Are you still obsessing over the carnival?"

"It's in four weeks," Layla said in her defense.

"But we've been over it and over it." Hazel moaned as she collapsed into the chair across from Layla. "And then you go over it and over it with Logan too."

"I like to be prepared."

Hazel watched her with her penetrating brown eyes. "There's a difference between prepared and crazy."

Layla huffed and opened the folder though she hadn't planned to look at it this morning. She wouldn't mention to Hazel that she'd been out to Steeple Ridge three times now just to "check on something."

"Let's go get our nails done this week," Hazel said. "You want to?"

Layla sighed and looked up in her friend's eyes. "Yeah, I want to."

"I didn't mean to imply you were being too…over-the-top with the winter carnival. It's a big event to plan solo." Hazel flashed her an apologetic smile and left Layla's office.

Layla watched her go, realizing that all her intensity—all the things Rick had told her she needed to stop doing—still existed within her. She left the folder where it sat and left the office. She caught Aria just as she was entering the back room where they kept their therapy dogs and the strays that were brought in.

"When's the first appointment?" she asked.

"Our nine o'clock just cancelled. Buster got in the back-yard again, and he was a muddy mess. So Gina's taking him to the dog groomer instead of here. He'll come tomorrow."

"So I have what? Thirty minutes?"

Aria glanced down at her clipboard. "Tina will be here in thirty minutes, yes."

Tina, a tiny little shih tzu, could wait if she had to. Layla vowed to hurry, but she needed a few more minutes to herself. She zipped out the back door and into her car, setting it toward the little church on Rooster Avenue.

Once inside, she took a deep, deep breath and calmed her heart beat. Since she'd invited Logan to Thanksgiving dinner with her family, she'd been praying more often and more fervently than she had in years. And she'd found more peace and more comfort than God had ever given her.

Lord, she started. *I know it's really early in my relationship with Logan. But please help me to have a clear mind concerning him. Guide my feet and actions. Calm my troubled soul.*

She kept her eyes closed and simply listened to the silence, hoping to hear the voice of God. She never had heard a physical voice, but sometimes she truly believed He was speaking to her. Thoughts would come into her mind—thoughts she didn't think belonged to her. Answers were given in simple feelings of right or wrong.

But now, she got nothing.

As the minutes passed, uncertainty crept in. Then confusion. And finally frustration. She couldn't understand why God would leave her hanging now, when He'd been so merciful previously.

Is it me? she wondered. *Am I being too intense about this?* An image of her red notebook with the words WEDDING PLANNER written on the front entered her mind. Maybe she was being a little too intense. It wasn't like Logan had proposed. And he'd be leaving town for two years.

Suddenly, a thought she'd never had popped into her head.

Maybe you should figure out how to go with him.

Layla jumped from the pew and headed toward the rectangle of light at the back of the chapel. She'd just entered the lobby when Pastor Gray said, "Layla?"

She turned to find him standing in the mouth of the hallway behind him. "Good morning, Pastor Gray."

"What are you doing here?" He glanced toward the chapel like others would follow her.

"Just praying. I feel…it feels nice here. It's quiet. Peaceful. I can really feel things when I'm here."

Pastor Gray smiled and leaned against the wall. "This church is a special place, that's for sure." He glanced into her rafters, a knowing smile on his face. "Did you find what you were looking for?"

"Sort of." Layla sighed, her earlier frustration roaring back. "Why doesn't God give us all the pieces we need? I swear, sometimes He just gives me one crumb at a time, and I'm left to wander through the woods, hoping and praying that I'm going in the right direction."

Pastor Gray chuckled. "Yes, He certainly does do that."

"It's frustrating."

"I know all about it." He moved toward the chapel and asked, "Do you have a minute?"

Layla had about ten left, so she joined him on the back row. He didn't say anything for what felt like hours. Then he finally said, "If God gave us all the pieces, there would be no need for faith."

"Sometimes faith is hard to have," Layla whispered. She didn't want to say it too loudly for some reason. "I have faith, Pastor. I do. But I—" She cut off, not sure she needed to get into all the particulars in that moment.

"It's hard to act without knowing what will come of it," he said. "Sometimes we get hurt. Sometimes we fall down. Sometimes we get lost for a time. But no matter what, we're never worse off when we act in faith." With that, he patted her knee the way her grandfather used to, stood, and left her sitting in the chapel.

Layla let his words sift through her brain. *We're never worse off when we act in faith.*

So she'd gotten one piece when she wanted the whole pie. *Time to act,* she thought as she stood and went back to the clinic.

CHAPTER
FIFTEEN

Logan watched Layla while she made dinner. Her phone went off every other second, and none of the messages brought a smile to her face. He finally got up from where he sat on the couch and asked, "Who's texting?"

"My stupid sisters," she grumbled, flipping her phone face down and stirring the browning ground beef on the stove with a little too much vigor.

"What did you send them this time?" He chuckled though he probably shouldn't have. But he'd endured several tastings of very disgusting pumpkin pie, and well, maybe Layla deserved some of what she was getting from her sisters.

She spun toward him, wooden spoon brandished. "You can't laugh at me if I tell you. And you can't say I should've done something different."

Logan grinned at her and wrapped his hands around

her waist. "What was it?" He placed a kiss on the skin just above the collar of her blouse. She shivered in his arms though her heater worked just fine. He grinned and kissed her closer to her ear.

"I sent them a list of acceptable conversation topics."

Logan couldn't help it. He tipped his head back and laughed. "I'm not laughing at you," he said around the still bubbling chuckles. "It's just—do you really think we won't have anything to talk about?"

She turned back to the stove, but not before he saw the wounded look on her face. "I haven't brought a man home in ten years, Logan."

"I know that. They know that. Everyone already knows that."

"My dad is a scholar."

"So you've said." He wrapped his arms around her and inched up behind her. "Layla."

"I just like to know how things are going to go," she said, stirring stirring stirring.

He took the wooden spoon from her and set it on the counter beside the stove. He turned her in his arms. "It's going to go fine. I'll like them, and they'll like me." He wished he felt as confident as he sounded. Truth was, he had no idea what he'd talk about with Layla's calculus-teaching father. He wasn't sure if her mother would like him or deem him unworthy of her daughter. He didn't have an education, a place to live, or anything to really offer someone as polished and smart as Layla.

He turned away from her and from his doubts. He'd never minded that he hadn't gone to college. No one he'd dated had either. Layla hadn't ever made him feel inferior to her, though she'd been to school for a decade and now practiced veterinary medicine at a successful clinic.

And that was another sticking point. What if they asked him about the dog training classes? What would he say then? *Yeah, I'm moving to California, and Layla…I don't know what Layla's going to do.*

He snuck a glance at her. Maybe he could ask her what she was going to do. He desperately wanted her to come with him. At the same time, it was still months and months away, and he hadn't even submitted his application yet. Darren had been bugging him about it, but Logan hadn't gotten online and taken care of it yet.

Maybe it was the stress of preparing for a trip to Boston. He still needed to talk to Tucker about taking the time off, something else Darren had been hounding him about. All at once, Logan felt like someone had dumped a load of bricks on his shoulders. He returned to Layla's couch, ready to stop being an adult for just a few minutes.

The next morning, Logan found Tucker and Missy in the office in the barn. "Hey, can I talk to you guys for a minute?"

"Sure, come on in." Tucker pointed to something on a piece of paper, and Missy said, "No, they came two weeks ago."

Tucker exhaled, his own problems clearly a burden to him, and looked at Logan. "What can we help you with?"

"Layla asked me to go to Boston with her for Thanksgiving. Could you guys survive without me for a few days?"

Missy stepped around the desk, her eyes set on laser-mode. "You're going to meet her family?"

"Yeah." Logan stuffed his hands in his pockets and tried to appear calm. Like this was no big deal. Like he met a woman's parents every other weekend.

"Wow," Tucker said. "That's huge."

"Sh," Missy said, shooting him a sharp look. "It's not huge. It's normal."

"We were engaged before I took you to New York."

"And you met my family on our first date."

"That wasn't a date," he said with a twinkle in his eye. "Remember how you told me we hadn't actually gone on any dates when I tried to kiss you?" He looked at Logan and shook his head. "The woman said she doesn't kiss on the first date. And here I thought we'd been out loads of times."

"Buying feed doesn't count as a date."

Tucker slung his arm around his wife. "It does now."

"It does not." She scowled at him but when she faced Logan again, she wore a smile.

"Well, Layla tried to break up with me after three and a half dates," he said.

"Three and a half?" Tucker asked. "How did you manage to go on half a date?"

"We doubled with Darren and Farrah."

Tucker blinked and then laughed. Missy elbowed him

and said, "We'll be fine without you for a few days, Logan. Have fun in Boston."

He tipped his hat and ducked out of the office, wanting to have fun, but unsure if it would actually happen.

———

THE DAY OF DEPARTURE CAME, AND LAYLA WAS DRIVING OUT to the farm to pick him up. Logan waited for her on the front porch, his suitcase at his feet and his stomach somewhere down in his boots. Why either of them had thought this visit was a good idea, he wasn't sure. Knowing Layla, she probably had a list to go over on the three-hour drive.

The thought made him smile. First, that he knew Layla so well. Second, that he got to spend the next three hours with her in the car. He used to love road trips with his family, and his parents had taken them to Yellowstone National Park, the Oregon coast, and even up to Banff in Canada.

It was what came after those three hours that he was worried about. Layla too, if her facial expression when she arrived was any indication.

"You look like you've seen a ghost." He lifted his suitcase into her trunk and swept a quick kiss across her cheek. "Everything okay?"

Silently, she handed him her phone.

"What's this?" He glanced at her and then it.

She swiped to unlock the device and then opened her texts. She had thirty-two unread messages in a group text. Thirty-two.

"Wow." He looked at her. "You want me to read these?"

"I had to mute the conversation," she said, a heavy note of bitterness in her tone. "They're driving me nuts."

"Maybe you should've taken someone home before now."

"They're going to ask you when we're getting married." Layla clenched her arms around her midsection and crunched her teeth together. "No matter what I say, my mother thinks she has a right to know."

Logan's throat turned dry, and though it was much too cold to stand around outside, chatting, he couldn't seem to get his legs to move.

"That's how I feel." Layla walked away from the car. "You're still okay to drive?"

Logan grunted and got behind the wheel. He drove back to town, past Layla's, past the Tonic Barn, and right out of Island Park before he asked, "What should I tell them?"

"About what?"

"Us getting married."

Layla's gaze on the side of his face felt scorching hot. "I don't know."

"Do you see yourself getting married?" he asked.

"Eventually."

Logan adjusted his grip on the steering wheel, the question he wanted—no, *needed*—to ask sitting right on his tongue. He gave himself a few more seconds to bottle up the emotions running wild through him. "Will you come to California with me when I go to do my dog training program?" He wouldn't let himself look at her.

"For the seven-week certification?"

"No, Layla. For the two years of classes until I earn my degree." He swallowed and it felt like he'd eaten glass for breakfast. "I want you to come to California with me, and in order to do that, I reckon we oughta be married." He looked at her, not comforted by the paleness of her face or the way her mouth had dropped open.

"You don't have to answer right now," he said quickly. In fact, he didn't want her to answer right now. If she did, he'd get a hearty *no*—and she might break up with him again.

"It's not until next fall. Months from now."

"Months," she echoed, and Logan decided now would be a great time to switch on the radio. She eventually thawed and started singing along, and by the time they arrived in Boston, the equilibrium between them had evened.

Her parents lived on the top floor of a sprawling apartment building, but Logan wouldn't be staying there. Her mother had put him in one of the rooms they had for college students, claiming there wouldn't be a roommate and it would be clean and ready for him. So he left his suitcase in the car and claimed Layla's bag in one hand and her hand in his other.

They stepped and breathed together. Once off the elevator, she met his gaze. "You ready for this?"

"Are you?"

"No way." She smiled, but it didn't reach her eyes and the corners didn't lift as high as they usually did. "Just...be you. You'll charm the pants right off of them."

"And you be you."

Fear paraded across her face. She turned to face the door and knocked at the same time she entered the apartment. "Mom? Dad? We're here."

Layla had obviously gotten her simplistic design preferences from her family, as they had comfortable furniture in the living room but not much else. No hutch with old pictures and knick knacks. A grouping of family pictures lined the wall down the hall and into the great room, where Layla found her sisters.

They squealed and jumped up from the couch while her mom said, "I didn't hear you get here." She met Logan's eyes and dusted her hands on her apron. "You must be Layla's boyfriend, Logan. Come in, come in." She was blonde like Layla, but bone thin with a long face and even longer limbs. She wore a smile the size of Texas, though, and Logan basked in the warmth of it.

He was already in, so he didn't know where else to go. She embraced him, so he went with it and hugged her back. "Very nice to meet you, ma'am."

"Oh, don't call me ma'am. My name's Callie. Greg's here somewhere." She turned toward a wall and yelled, "Greg! The kids are here!"

Logan had no idea what she was doing, but a man at least as tall as him came down another hall, saying, "I heard them. You don't need to yell."

"I wasn't sure if you were asleep or not."

"Logan." Her dad extended his hand, and Logan shook it.

"Sir."

"Greg," her mom corrected.

No way Logan was calling the man Greg. He was twice as wide as Logan, and his shoes surely had to be custom-made. He wore a pair of black slacks that could probably sail a boat on a windy day and a shirt the color of red apples.

Layla bustled over to him with "Hey, Daddy," and gave him a semi-awkward side hug. "You guys, this is Logan."

Logan received more hugs from the sisters—Alice, the youngest, and Vanessa, the middle child. Neither of them were married, and Logan wondered how often the Guyman's had experienced this kind of thing before. Probably about as often as he had.

Layla sat on the couch and Logan joined her. The sisters retook their places, and Greg sat in the double-wide recliner. Her mom continued to work in the kitchen, but she called, "So, Logan. Have you and Layla talked about getting married?"

"Mom," Vanessa said in a warning tone.

Layla gave an exaggerated sigh, but Logan just grinned, the words he should say suddenly in his mind. "I've asked her, but she's still tryin' to decide."

The look she gave him was priceless, and Logan really wanted to know what she'd say now that the ball was in her court.

CHAPTER
SIXTEEN

Layla stared at Logan for several seconds before elbowing him in the side. He grunted but didn't flinch. *Stupid, strong cowboy*, she thought.

"He didn't ask me to marry him," she said. "We've talked about it a couple of times, that's all."

Once. They'd talked about it *once*, and only because Alice had warned her that her mother was on the marriage warpath and Layla had wanted Logan to be prepared. She certainly hadn't expected him to throw her under the bus. She gave him a glare and he simply grinned wider.

She didn't like the way her dad stared at Logan, never flinching, never looking away. He wore a strange half-smile that annoyed her, so she didn't glance in his direction again.

"We've only been dating for a few months," Layla added, unsure as to why she felt like she needed to explain further. She'd said all this on the phone with them. Her mom called every Sunday after all.

"What do you do for a living, Logan?" her father asked, and Layla shifted on the couch. She'd already told them all what he did.

Her mom came rushing over. "He's a cowboy, Greg. Layla already told us that."

Logan leaned closer to her. "How much have you told them?" he whispered.

"Everything," she hissed back.

He settled back into the couch. "I work at Steeple Ridge Farm," he said. "I train horses, and fix fences, and apparently I'm going to drive a sleigh come Christmas."

Her dad lifted his eyebrows. "I've never pictured Layla with a cowboy." He finally tore his eyes from Logan, but Layla didn't like the way her father looked at her either. "You do know she's a veterinarian, right? She went to school for nine years."

"She's a fantastic vet," Logan said, a nearly silent vein of tension in his voice. Layla knew him well enough to hear it, to notice the way his muscles tensed beside her. "She's putting on a winter carnival for all her clients. They love her."

"Do you love her?"

"Dad." Layla shot to her feet, dragging Logan with her. "Let's go put your bag in your apartment."

"Don't go," her mom said.

Alice and Vanessa started lecturing her father, but Layla felt very close to tears. "I just need the key, Mom."

She held out her hand. Her mom looked back and forth between her and her dad, her hands fisting in her apron.

"The key, Mom." Her fingers gripped Logan's, and he squeezed her hand.

"It's okay, Layla."

"No." She spun to him and then to her father. "You promised you wouldn't act like this." She added her voice to her sisters', who still hadn't stopped giving him a verbal whipping.

Alice ended with, "You did the same thing to Brandon. This is why none of us are married," her chest heaving and a line of tears running down her face.

Her father just stood and walked out of the living room, going back down the hall to his study. He hadn't apologized.

"He's just proud of you." Her mom handed her a key.

"He thinks no one is good enough for me." Layla started for the door. "He's the reason I haven't dated since Rick." She heaved open the apartment door and left. She made it to the elevator before she realized Logan hadn't come with her. She didn't even know the moment she'd dropped his hand.

She swiped at her tears and got on the elevator, Logan's voice filtering down the hall to her. "I'm so sorry, ma'am. I'll see what I can do."

The elevator doors closed, separating her and Logan, though the sound of his cowboy boots on the tile came closer at a rapid clip.

She exploded out of the building, the air inside too

toxic to breathe. Her father had said horrible things about Rick, and Layla realized that she'd invented her Dating Rules after the trip home after Rick's break-up.

Her father had been livid, and he'd told her that she deserved someone as strong as she was, as dedicated to his work, as loving and kind.

Logan was all of those things. Just because he didn't have a medical degree didn't make him any less of a person. She turned to go back and tell her father all of those things and how he didn't get to influence her any more with his staring and his rude questions.

She collided with a very solid object. A very solid object whose arms came around her and kept her from falling.

"Whoa," Logan said. "Slow down."

"I need—I need—" Her breath heaved in her chest. "I have to go tell my father how wonderful you are."

He shook his head, his face so serious it made Layla stall. "No, Layla. Let's walk." He turned her around and went down the sidewalk. He held her hand but didn't grip it, making her come with him.

"I'm so sorry, Logan," she said.

"It's fine."

"It's not fine," she said. "My father—well." The fight started to ebb away. "That's how he is. He won't apologize."

"He'll just look at me like I'm inadequate." Logan glanced at her. "Is that it?"

"That's about it."

He exhaled, and Layla imagined the next thirty years.

Thirty Thanksgivings. Thirty Christmases where her father stared at Logan, said rude things, and disappeared down the hall. He didn't have parents to visit on holidays, and Layla started to think of excuses for why they couldn't come to Boston for turkey and mashed potatoes.

Logan stopped at the corner and scanned the sky. She gave him the time he needed to think, to organize what he wanted to say. He didn't speak.

"Tell me what you're thinking," she said, sliding both her hands around him.

"I'm thinking your father is right." He wouldn't look at her, and Layla hated that. Hated it with every fiber of her being.

"My father is not right."

"I'm not good enough for you, Layla. Maybe in…." He exhaled. "Maybe when I have an education and a real job."

"You have a real job," she argued. "You're really good at what you do."

"I feel…I feel inadequate. In so many ways, not just with you. I—" His voice caught, and Layla held him tight.

"I have never once implied that you're not good enough for me, have I?" she asked.

He shook his head. "No, Layla. You're too nice to do that."

"It's not because I'm nice, Logan."

"I need a minute." He released her hand and walked away from her. Layla had never felt so much in a single moment before. Anger at her father. Complete despair at watching her boyfriend leave her standing by herself on the sidewalk. Frustration at her family. Dread at having to go back to that apartment. Agony that Logan believed he wasn't good enough for her.

More tears fell, and Layla turned away from Logan and walked in the opposite direction.

CHAPTER
SEVENTEEN

Logan had never felt as awful as he did walking the streets of Boston. With every other step, his pulse boomed at him to *go back to Layla! Make sure Layla is all right.*

He didn't go back.

Because for the first time since his parents had died, Logan had truly known he could be more than he currently was. And he didn't like the feelings of inadequacy. The weight he now carried that he needed to do more with his life.

Sure, he'd been feeling it for a few months, had looked into the dog training programs at Bergin. But he hadn't submitted his application, because he wasn't sure he should go to school. And the real reason was because he didn't want to lose Layla.

She provided such a well of encouragement that Logan

wasn't sure he could go to school without her. He'd never been particularly book smart, and he simply couldn't leave her in Vermont while he went to California.

What do I do? The question ran in an endless loop in his mind, and when he saw a tall building with a cross on the front, he ducked inside. He didn't see anyone, and he stayed for several minutes, trying to work through solutions in his mind.

In the end, he left the church without any solid answers, so he called Darren. "Hey," his brother said. "Did you make it to Boston?"

"Yeah." Logan sighed. "I'm in Boston."

"Something's wrong."

"Yeah, something's wrong." It took Logan several seconds to work up the strength to tell his brother what had happened at the apartment. He ended with, "So I'm out walking by myself, and I don't know what to do."

"You haven't submitted your application to Bergin yet?"

"That's what you're worried about?"

Darren growled and then exhaled. "Farrah just got here, so this will have to be brief. It will sound harsh, but I trust that when you think about it, you'll understand. Logan, you're stuck. You're not doing anything. You don't have a plan for the future, so you have no plans. If you knew you were going to California in the fall, you'd make plans with Layla. She knows you have no plans, even though you talk a big game. So she's not going to commit, because hey, no one wants their heart broken."

Darren took a breath, and his words had stunned Logan into a standstill.

"So make some blasted plans, Logan. You won't die. Submit your application. Tell Layla you love her and you want her to come with you to California. See if she can make some plans to do that with you. But, without any solid plans…. Never gonna happen."

"Thanks, Darren," Logan said woodenly, unsure of how he felt. Numb, for sure. His brother's lecture steamrolled through his thoughts. *Tell Layla you love her.*

"Farrah's here. I'll call you later. Just think about it, and don't be too mad at me." Darren hung up, and Logan stared at the phone for several long seconds. Could Darren be right? Was he in love with Layla?

Logan shoved his phone in his pocket and glanced around like someone had heard him say he loved her. He wasn't sure how he felt, and he knew he needed to figure it out fast. He found a bench and sent a message to Layla.

Let's go to lunch. Take my bag to my room.

She asked where he was, and he texted her the names of the streets. Twenty minutes later, she pulled up in her car. Logan heaved himself off the bench and into the passenger seat. "Hey." He looked out the window, wondering what he should say first.

Layla drove, turning down this street and then that one until she pulled into the parking lot at a diner. "This place has phenomenal chicken fried steak."

"Phenomenal, huh?" Logan asked, starting to get some of his old self back.

She watched him with worried eyes and a smile. "I should've warned you about my family."

He shook his head. "They're fine. I just—like I said, I'm a little lost." He twisted toward her. "I haven't submitted my application to Bergin yet. But I'm going to as soon as we get back to Island Park."

She nodded, her throat constricting when she swallowed. "So you'll start next fall."

"Yes." He worked up the courage he needed, but it didn't quite make it all the way to his voice, because it sounded too high when he said, "I want you to come. Have you thought about it?"

"Logan." She sounded like he was annoying her. She got out of the car and he joined her on the sidewalk leading up to the diner.

"Too soon," he said. "Okay."

"It's not too soon." She opened the door and let him enter first. "It's just that there's a lot I'd have to do to be ready to leave Paws & Claws by fall."

He waited while the hostess took them to a booth. "Would you do it?"

"You haven't even gotten in."

Ah, so Darren was right. Layla wasn't going to sell her clinic, or turn it over to someone else, without a serious commitment from Logan.

"So, if I submit my application, and I get in, and I buy you a diamond ring, would you come with me to California?"

Layla squeaked as she sucked in a breath. "Is that a proposal?"

Logan scoffed and opened the menu. "Of course not. You think I'm so much of a ruffian, I wouldn't even get down on one knee?" He shook his head. "I swear, sometimes you don't know me at all." He flashed her a grin so she'd know he was kidding and went back to the menu. His insides boiled and the thought of eating didn't sit well in his gut.

"Well, Logan, if you did all of those things, I would figure out what to do with Paws & Claws."

"You shouldn't sell it," he said. "Hire someone to run it for a couple of years. We'll be back."

"Right, because you bought a lot by the barn."

"And I like living in Island Park."

"Maybe you won't be able to work from Island Park."

"I'm sure it'll work out." He lowered his menu and finally met her eye. "Don't you think it'll work out, Layla?" He reached across the table and took both of her hands in his.

"I think sometimes things have to be planned to work out the way we want them to."

Logan groaned. "You sound just like Darren."

She sniffed and cocked her head from side to side. "Well, at least one of you is thinking ahead."

"You do that for me, Layla." He chuckled at the horrified look on her face.

"I do not," she said.

"All right," he said, not wanting to argue. But he had to admit that he felt a little less lost when he was with Layla. She knew where she was going, and what she was doing, and how every little piece fit into the puzzle of life. Logan knew there was a puzzle, and that it was filled with amazing colors and pictures. But he still didn't quite know how he fit, and if Layla would be right beside him when he figured it out.

CHAPTER
EIGHTEEN

Layla endured Thanksgiving dinner with her family. Everyone stuck to the approved topics she'd sent out, even her father. He didn't ask any more questions. In fact, he hardly spoke at all before disappearing down the hall again.

Her mother brought out three pies once dinner had settled. "Chocolate, pumpkin, and pecan," she announced, proudly beaming down at the baked goods. "Who wants what?"

Logan took chocolate, the way Layla knew he would. She chose pecan, and he gave her a curious look but said nothing. They ate their pie on the balcony with Alice and Vanessa, who had been good-natured and supportive through everything.

But Layla wasn't sorry to leave Boston in her rear-view mirror. Logan didn't seem to be either. She didn't apologize again. He'd just say, "It's fine," again and she'd be left wondering if it really was okay. Again.

They'd originally planned to stay until Sunday and drive home after church, but they pulled into Island Park around lunchtime on Friday. Downtown bustled with shoppers carrying their purchases and loitering on Main Street because the eateries were full. Layla's stomach growled, but she didn't want to wait in line.

"We could go to Burlington," she suggested. "It's another twenty-five minutes, but maybe the lunch rush will be over by then."

Logan said, "Sure," and set the car north. As he drove past the Sports Complex, Layla couldn't help thinking of Ben and Rae's wedding. She'd been reunited with Logan there, had seen that interested spark in his eyes that night before he'd disappeared, was glad he'd acted on his feelings for a second time.

She reached over and took his hand in hers with a sigh.

"You okay?" he asked.

"Just fine." She leaned her head back and closed her eyes. She'd been thinking a lot about moving all the way across the country to California. The very idea intimidated her, and she needed a new notebook. A new set of colorful gel pens. And some time to make a plan.

She imagined herself engaged, and then married, to Logan. Warmth filled her, and she remembered her morning at the church when she'd felt like she should go with him. She hadn't quite acted at that time, as Logan hadn't expressly asked her to go with him. But he had now, and Layla's fingers itched to start making lists and sketching out plans for who would take care of the rescues once she left. Could Aria serve the town as a technician? Or would Layla need to hire a full-fledged veterinarian? Her mind spun, and before she knew it, Logan had navigated them to a buffet near the movie theater.

"They have salad," he said. "And you didn't answer when I asked you where you wanted to go. Did you fall asleep?"

"Yes," she said as he lifted her wrist to his lips and kissed her, because it was easier than telling him that she'd simply lost herself to her fantasies of a life with him but without her clinic.

———

A WEEK PASSED, AND LAYLA HAD ALMOST FORGOTTEN ABOUT the disastrous trip to Boston, when Logan showed up wearing his serious face again. She pressed the point of her pen into the chart she was finishing and asked, "What's wrong?"

"I got into Bergin," he said. He didn't move toward Bones's leash the way he normally did. He didn't come closer to her and press a kiss to her lips the way he normally did. Everything about this Thursday stop to get the dogs for their therapy felt skewed.

"Well, that's good news," Layla said cautiously. "Why do you look like Rambo died?" She sucked in a breath and covered her mouth. "Did Rambo die?"

"No." He shook his head. "Rambo's fine. I—I submitted my application, the way I said I would. They called this morning with a 'great opportunity.'" He made finger quotes around the last two words, and Layla realized she was speaking with an angry version of Logan Buttars. She'd never seen him get angry before. Frustrated, sure. Serious even. But never angry.

"What's the great opportunity?" Her heart galloped around in her chest, dislodging some vital organs and making her whole body hurt.

"They just had someone drop out of the program that starts in January. They wondered if I could be in California on January eighth."

Layla dropped her pen now, her jaw following. "January eighth?"

Logan's mask cracked and his shoulders fell. "Darren says I should go. There's nothing holding me back." He finally swept toward her, all his muscles working together to bring him to her in only a few strides. He took her in his arms and gazed down at her. "But I can't leave here without you. Layla, I'm—I—Layla, I'm in love with you."

A smile burst onto her face. "I love you, too, Logan."

He kissed her then, and Layla basked in the love she felt flowing from him to her. She freely gave it back, sure she could grow old with him and be happy. She had no idea love like this existed. No idea she'd ever let herself get this far with a man.

"So you'll come to California?" he whispered. He kneaded her closer and lighted kisses along her jaw and neck. "I know it's only a month, but you'll come?"

The pleading undercurrent in his voice made Layla

stiffen and pull back from him. "Logan, I don't think I can be ready to leave my clinic in only a month."

He stepped back, the dark look entering his eyes again. "Of course not. I know that. I do."

"Are you going to go?"

Logan inhaled, his chest puffing out. He released his breath and nodded. "I'm going to go." He hooked his thumb over his shoulder. "I'll talk to you later." He gathered the dog's leashes and said, "Let's go," to them without attaching the lines. They went with him, because they loved him.

Layla wondered why she couldn't do the same. A sob worked its way out of her throat, because she strongly suspected that she wouldn't see Logan Buttars again.

Sure enough, he didn't come to her office when he returned Ginger Ale and Bones. He didn't call or text that day or night. She texted him after eating her lonely dinner with, *When are you moving?*

Over New Year's.

Could I come in a few months? Layla looked at her message and couldn't bring herself to send it. She didn't want to beg him. She wanted him to ask her to come when she could. To show up in his truck and hold her before he left.

She also knew he wouldn't do either one. Logan didn't make plans, not even to stop by and make sure she knew he loved her before he crossed the country and left her here.

He might ask, she thought, thumbing off the message.

He'd asked her to come already. He'd said he couldn't leave here without her.

"So maybe he won't." She glanced up and found Sweet Pea panting only a few feet away. "Right, Sweet? Maybe he won't leave town without me."

I have your Santa costume, she sent instead.

About that....

Layla stared at the words, her heartbeat accelerating until it sped dangerously. She hit call, needing to hear Logan tell her right to her face that he wasn't going to be Santa and drive the sleigh, something they'd talked about dozens of times and that she'd been planning on for months.

"Layla."

"Are you saying you aren't coming to the winter carnival?"

"Layla," he said again, this time drawing her name out a little longer.

"Because it's in one week, Logan, and I need you."

"Layla."

"I based my flyers around that horse-drawn carriage," she said, her panic pouring into her sentences now. "And it's supposed to snow all week, which will make the sleigh ride extra magical, and I went and bought extra bells, Logan. Extra bells."

"I'm sorry I can't do it. But don't worry," he practically yelled. She sucked back in her next words to listen to him. "I asked Darren to do it, and he said he would."

"Darren?" She didn't want Darren to do it.

"We're twins, Lay. Call him by my name if you put that on the flyer."

"I put Santa Claus on the flyer." Layla felt like she was floating, like this conversation wasn't reality. "Logan." She swallowed and employed her confidence. "Are we broken up?"

He sighed, a long, drawn-out sound that made Layla feel like an argumentative teenager. "You said you couldn't come to California."

"No," she said. "I said I couldn't come to California in a month."

"That's when I'm going."

"But you could still drive the sleigh," she said. "You'll be here next weekend, won't you?"

"Yes."

"So?" she challenged.

"Layla," he said. "This is—this is all just a little bit too much for me."

"What is? Moving across the country in a month? That's a lot for anyone."

"I'm sorry," he said. "I wanted you to come with me, and you said you couldn't."

"It's in a month!" Layla said. Why wouldn't he ask her to come later? Had he really not thought of it?

"Maybe—" she started but he said, "Everything is happening too fast, and I can only focus on one thing at a time. I'm really sorry, Layla, but that thing right now is getting myself to California in time to start their program so I don't lose any more time."

"Any more time?" she asked. "What does that mean?"

"It means my entire life has been a waste," he said, his voice as loud as she'd ever heard it. "I'm almost twenty-nine-years-old, and I've not done one thing with my life. Not one thing that anyone cares about. This is me doing that. I can make a real difference with service dog therapy. A real difference."

Layla didn't know how to respond to his outburst. "I—I didn't know you needed to make a difference."

"Everything your father said—the stuff he implied—is right. I'm nothing. I'm nobody. I don't even have a house to live in." He chuckled, but it didn't contain an ounce of happiness. "I sat outside the clinic for an hour after dropping off the dogs. I wanted to come in. I wanted to ask you to come with me whenever you can get out to California. But then I realized how selfish that makes me, and it's better for me if it's just a clean break. That's why I can't do the Santa sleigh for you."

"You are not nobody," she said, her brain reeling with everything he'd said. She needed more time to make sense of all of it, but her mind stalled on the fact that Logan thought her father was right.

"I have to go," he said, the words echoing in her ears. "'Bye, Layla."

It took her almost a minute to realize he'd hung up. And only a moment for her absolute anger to flood every cell in her body. Her fingers shook as she dialed her mother, and she barked, "Put Dad on the phone," when her mom answered.

As she waited for her father to get on the line, her heart broke and a rush of tears streamed down her face.

She ended the call and curled into the couch, sure Logan would call any moment and say he was coming up. Any moment. Any moment….

CHAPTER
NINETEEN

Logan hated winter. He hated the snow, even though it fell magically around him as he stamped his way toward the back barn. He hated the sight of the sleigh sitting out by the arena. He hated that he'd broken up with Layla, backed out of his agreement to be her Santa Claus, and that he wouldn't be going to California with her at his side.

Only one thing made sense anymore. When Bergin had called and offered him a spot in the January courses, he'd practically heard the voice of the Lord telling him to take it. He'd prayed about Layla, and God had been decidedly silent on that front. Logan couldn't make her decisions for her. He'd said he loved her. He'd asked her to come with him.

But deep down, he'd known she wouldn't come in January. She needed a lot more time to make her plans, pack her apartment, and take care of her clinic.

He ducked into the barn after casting the sleigh one last look. He'd have to make sure he sequestered himself in the farmhouse during the carnival. Seeing Layla again before he left Island Park would be too painful.

The thought of the lot he'd bought at the Tonic Barn made his feet freeze to the floor. What was he doing? Breaking up with Layla, planning to skip church for the next month, hiding at the farm? What would he do when he returned to Island Park to "build his life"? Avoid her forever? Hope another vet had moved to town so he could take Rambo there?

"Idiot," he muttered to himself. He'd made a real mess of things—all because he hadn't thought everything through before acting. Because Logan didn't make a plan for anything. He acted with how he felt in the moment.

And now he'd lost Layla because of it.

He tried to hold onto the knowledge that getting his degree was absolutely right. If only being with Layla didn't feel the same way. Why had God given him two new pieces, great pieces, for his life and not provided a way for him to make them fit together?

Logan was so tired of thinking about things. He wanted to work so he didn't have to think. So he shoveled, and fed, and bathed, and shuffled horses from stall to stall. Back in the farmhouse, he made dinner for everyone, and then cleaned the upstairs bathroom. All so he could collapse into bed and be so tired he didn't have time to mull things over. Again.

And so Logan worked. He knew how to do that. Knew how to clean kitchen tile until it sparkled. Knew how to scrub grime from the tiny ledges on baseboards. Knew how to pack boxes. Knew how to search for an apartment online.

It seemed impossible that only six days had passed, as they seemed to take a year for each twenty-four hour cycle.

"So you're really not doing the winter carnival?" Darren asked as he set the coffee maker to percolate.

Logan slid onto the barstool, already tired and he'd just gotten up. "I don't know. I can't do it. I can't be around her and not be with her."

"That's your choice, bro." Darren put a gallon of milk on the counter and pulled out five or six boxes of cereal. He slid the paper bowls near the cornflakes and said, "Mornin', Cody," without looking away from Logan.

Logan glanced at the cowboy not related to him. "Do you think I could drive the sleigh and pretend to be you? Then there won't be any awkwardness."

Cody didn't look at him but Logan could tell he was listening.

"So you just want to torture yourself?" Darren filled a bowl with chocolate krispies and waited for Logan to answer.

"Yes," Logan said, reaching for his own bowl. He couldn't explain himself to Darren. He didn't even quite know why he wanted to be at the carnival without Layla knowing.

"She'll know it's you," Darren said.

"How?"

"I'm taller than you." He held himself higher as if that were true.

"You are not."

"I'm more mature." He flashed Logan a grin, and Logan wished he'd never told his brother about that conversation.

"Can I do it or not?"

"You think I want to drive a sleigh for two hours? Be my guest. I'll call Farrah and see if she wants to get together."

"How are you and Farrah getting along?" Logan asked.

"Great." Darren cast a long look at Cody and met Logan's eye again before excusing himself and heading up the stairs, his unmilked cereal still on the counter. Logan poured milk over the chocolate krispies and ate his brother's bowl of cereal while Cody waited for the coffee to finish.

An hour later, Logan sauntered out of the farmhouse wearing the Santa suit. He found Layla's car already in the guest lot and when he first caught sight of her, clipboard in hand, his heart exploded painfully in his chest.

Without his cowboy hat, he thought sure Layla wouldn't know the difference between him and Darren. Logan just needed to say very little and look a little surlier. He arranged his face into a semi-scowl and approached her. If she had x-ray vision, she'd be able to see his heart throbbing beneath the red fur.

"Mornin', Layla," he said in what he believed to be a very good Darren drawl. "We all set?"

She didn't glance up at him. "You're all set, Darren, yes. Sleigh rides will be departing from the main barn. People will line up over there."

"Great." He went back the way he'd come without allowing himself to take a deep drag of the air surrounding her. Darren wouldn't do that, and Logan didn't want to make this day harder for her than it surely already was.

The event started several minutes later, and dozens of people and their pets showed up at Steeple Ridge, including Tucker and Missy and Ben and Rae. Kids got their faces painted with snowflakes, and the scent of hot chocolate could probably be smelled in Burlington. Logan filled the sleigh time and time again. He said "ho ho ho!" and rang the jingle bells every time a ride started and ended. He did exactly what Layla had wanted him to.

And just like he'd expected, he was utterly exhausted by the end of the carnival. When he and Layla were dating, he'd expected to be able to hold her and tell her what a great job she'd done, and then take her to lunch.

Hidden behind Darren's personality, he put Paintbrush away and went to find Layla to check out. "All good?" he asked, his voice probably too gruff.

"Yes, thanks, Darren." She beamed up at him for less than a heartbeat. He wondered why she couldn't look at him, even when she thought him to be his twin. "You saved me. Merry Christmas."

"Merry Christmas," he said, the last word catching. He spun and strode away before Layla could look at him more fully and discover his deception. He made it outside the arena and paused, his chest heaving with the effort it took to be in the same space as her and not be hers. Not have her be his.

"Your choice," he muttered, repeating Darren's words.

But Logan didn't know how to fix what he'd done. Layla couldn't go with him to school in less than a month, and it was unfair to expect her to. Breaking up was the kind thing to do.

"Choosing her would be the kind thing to do." Logan pushed away from the fence and hurried back to the farmhouse, where Darren sat on the bottom stair, engaged in a phone conversation. It only took a moment for Logan to figure out that he was talking to Sam.

"They broke up," he said, and Logan glanced at him. "Yeah, he got into his program, and he's leaving in a few weeks. Layla can't go, so he thought they should just end things."

Judging by the disdainful look on his brother's face, Logan gathered that Darren didn't agree with his decision.

"I have no idea, Sam. I don't see why he couldn't just have asked her to come when she could. Layla's a great planner. She'd take things one at a time, make sure her clinic was all set, and then she'd follow him anywhere."

Logan scoffed and turned toward the kitchen, but Darren's voice wouldn't be silenced.

"You should see her look at him. She's in love with him. She'd go. He just needed to ask."

"I did ask," Logan said over his shoulder.

"No," Darren said. "He asked her to come with him next fall, and she seemed set to do that, at least according to him." He stood and came around Logan to face him. "So she can't go in January. Why not ask her to come when she can?"

"Because I don't want everything to be about me."

"Too late, Logan. Moving to California is all about you. It always has been." Darren spun away from him, but not before Logan saw the hurt in his brother's eyes.

"Darren," he said. "You've always said I should do this."

"Doesn't mean I'm happy about bein' left here by myself." His expression changed as he listened to whatever Sam was saying. "Yeah, Ben's still here, but it's not the same, Sam. Nothing's been the same since you left." He returned to the bottom step and sat heavily.

Logan felt the same notes of sadness in his heart that Darren carried in his voice.

"I know," Darren said. "I know.... You're right.... I'll tell him. Bye, Sam." Darren ended the call but remained on the bottom step. He sighed as he stood up. "He said you're stupid if you go to California without Layla. He said he did that, remember? And he was miserable and so was Bonnie. Said to think about that."

Logan knew he'd been foolish. What he didn't know was how to fix it.

"What do you already know that he said?"

"Nothing." Darren turned and went up the stairs, and Logan watched him go, realizing that for the first time, Darren hadn't told him everything.

Logan stood in the farmhouse, wondering how he could have his dog training program and the woman he loved. In the same place at the same time.

To get Layla back and still be able to start school in just a few weeks, Logan would need a plan. Determined, he walked down the hall and into the office Sam used to use.

Those duties had been turned back over to Tucker, and now this room sat empty most of the time.

A bookshelf remained, as did the desk, though it only held an unused speaker system and a printer. Logan grabbed a couple pieces of paper and sat at the desk, ready to make a plan that would win Layla over and end with him begging her to come to California whenever she could.

He picked up a pen and stared at the blank page. Nothing came. Logan literally had no idea how to make a plan, and the one person who could help him wasn't currently talking to him.

CHAPTER
TWENTY

Layla knocked on her neighbor's door with a loaf of bread in one hand and a jar of soup in the other. It didn't really sound like knocking. More like a two-pound loaf of bread banging against wood.

Meredith answered the door anyway, that holiday glow on her face and on the Christmas tree in the room behind her.

"Creamy chicken noodle," Layla announced in a falsely cheery voice. "And the nine-grain bread Danny loves."

"Layla brought dinner," she called behind her. She met Layla's eyes. "Again. Lay, what's going on?"

The nickname sent a shockwave through her. "Logan." Her throat closed around the rest of the sentence, because she couldn't speak about him without choking up.

"You guys broke up?" Meredith covered her mouth with one hand and passed the bread to her husband with the other. "Come in, Layla. Come eat with us."

She shook her head. "No, you guys enjoy. I already ate."

Meredith tilted her head to the side like she could see the lie on Layla's face. She hadn't been able to eat much more than toast lately, but she cooked as if she were feeding half the apartment building.

She also couldn't get over the fact that Logan really hadn't shown up to be her Santa Claus. He'd said he wouldn't, but she hadn't believed him. He'd committed to doing it, and she didn't want to think he was a person who went back on his promises.

But Darren had shown up. Darren had traded out his cowboy hat for a Santa cap. Darren had driven the sleigh and entertained her patrons.

And that stung deeper than Layla had anticipated.

"What are you doing for Christmas?" Meredith asked.

Layla shook herself from the winter carnival. The thought of going home for Christmas made her shudder. She thought of waking up on that sacred morning, alone in her apartment, and opening a gift she'd purchased for herself. That made her feel so much worse.

"So you'll come over here," Meredith said though Layla hadn't answered. "We'll have Belgian waffles with strawberries and whipped cream for breakfast, and watch *The Miracle on Thirty-Fourth Street*, and exchange gifts."

Relief washed through Layla, and a rush of affection for her friend. "Thanks, Mer." She backed up and turned to go back to her place, wondering how she could survive this holiday season without Logan.

She made it back to her apartment and sank onto the couch, her phone in her hand. She flipped through the pictures she'd taken at the winter carnival earlier that day. Pride filled her. She had put on a good event, and the people who'd come had enjoyed themselves. The pets had played together, the sleigh had run non-stop, and she'd drunk at least six cups of hot chocolate to keep herself from marching over to the farmhouse and asking to see Logan.

He probably wasn't even there, she told herself as she continued to look through her pictures. She'd put several of the best ones on her website tomorrow after church.

Church.

She froze.

Would Logan go to church?

Would Layla have to reorganize her entire life so she didn't run into him? There was only one grocery store in town, and though she'd never seen him there, he surely shopped there. She set her phone down and stared straight forward.

She would not reorganize her life. She'd go to church tomorrow, the way she normally did. She'd shop how she normally did, and she'd go to work as she normally did. If she ran into Logan, it wouldn't matter. Her heart was already in shreds, and most of the pieces were out at Steeple Ridge Farm.

She laid down on the couch, unable to get herself to go down the hall to her bedroom. She wasn't sure how the world could continue to revolve when Logan wasn't texting her, wasn't holding her hand, wasn't kissing her.

And she realized that her relationship with him had been so much more than her stint with Rick.

She'd stopped dating for ten years because of him. She wouldn't do that again. But she also didn't want anyone but Logan.

She stared, small ideas for how she could get him back planting themselves in her mind. But she didn't have the urge to get a notebook and start making plans. She needed to stop living her life according to a checklist.

"Starting now," she whispered as she closed her eyes.

———

THE NEXT MORNING, PASTOR GRAY STOOD AT THE PULPIT AND said, "This is the season of love. The Savior demonstrated great love for all those he came in contact with. One of the best ways to show love this holiday season is to be forgiving."

From her position near the front, Layla stiffened. She'd arrived very early to church and had managed to keep facing the front so she wouldn't have to see if Logan came with his family or not. The thought of being in the same building with him but not having him at her side burned her throat. She'd hoped Pastor Gray would say inspired things that would uplift and comfort her silent injuries.

But this sermon wasn't cooling her wounds. In fact, with everything the preacher said, Layla's anger grew.

She didn't want to pick someone in her life and forgive them. She wanted her father to feel guilty for planting negative ideas in Logan's head. She wanted to feel justified in her anger that Logan hadn't driven the sleigh the way he'd said he would.

When Pastor Gray said, "When we forgive, it is really us who benefits," Layla stood and marched out of the chapel. She didn't glance to the back right corner to see if Logan sat there. She was stronger than that.

Once free of the church, Layla just walked. She hated winter, and rarely spent much time outdoors from November to April, but she tugged her coat tighter around her body and kept her feet moving. If only her mind would stop, but it didn't.

Deep down, she understood the preacher's words. She had always been quick to forgive her father. She didn't hold grudges. She'd gotten over Rick quickly, even if his poisoned words had haunted her for years.

As she crossed Pheasant Drive, she finally understood the reason she'd been able to leave Rick behind so easily. She hadn't loved him. She hadn't been able to shed his words because they were what resonated with her.

She'd tried to be less her with Logan. She hadn't done a great job, and somewhere along the way, she'd stopped thinking about it. She wasn't even sure when that had happened.

I'm in love with you, Layla.

His words had looped through her mind for days. They wouldn't leave, much the same way Rick's hadn't.

She'd felt like she should prepare herself to go with him when he left for college. "It wasn't supposed to happen so soon," she said to the smoothie shop as she passed. "But I can still go."

She crossed Crow's Crescent and walked through the quiet neighborhood, each breath hanging in the air. "I'm still going to go."

Determined in her plan to make a plan to go to California by summer, Layla did an about-face and headed back to the church. She didn't go inside, though. She paused on the steps, her fingers curling around the door handle.

She'd come to a decision on one of her problems without realizing how much work it would take. Because not only did she need to find a replacement vet, train them, and get the clinic staff up-to-date before she left, she also needed to figure out how to forgive Logan.

––––––––––

LAYLA PRAYED OVER THE COURSE OF THE NEXT WEEK. LORD, help me to know what to do about the clinic. Could Aria manage the load?

Help me find the right person to manage the clinic.

Help me overcome my anger toward Logan.

The prayers went with her while she visited cats and dogs and even a pet ferret. Everyone kept telling her how wonderful the carnival had been and that they hoped she'd do it again next year. She didn't have the heart to tell them she wouldn't be in town next year.

As soon as she started looking for a replacement vet, though, she wouldn't be able to hide it. For now, she hadn't told anyone. But she did ask the building inspector to come and let her know what repairs the clinic needed.

He was scheduled to come on Monday afternoon. And she had plans to talk to Hazel and Aria at their standing lunch at the country club.

She'd packed a few boxes of summer clothes and done a walk-through of her apartment. Since the building was so new, she didn't need to do a lot to get it ready to sell. All the extra tasks kept her mind and body busy, something she also prayed to thank the Lord for. Though the reason for her increased workload was Logan, she didn't think about him nearly as much as she had that first week after their break-up.

"So, you've been unusually cheerful this week," Aria said after they'd gone through the line and loaded their salad plates.

"Am I not allowed to be happy?" Layla pushed her lettuce around her plate, gathering the appetite that had failed her recently.

Aria exchanged a glance with Hazel. "It's just that…the first week after you broke up with Logan, you walked around like the living dead. This week…you're different." She ripped off a piece of her roll and buttered it.

"I wanted to talk to you guys about something." Layla put down her fork. "I'm going to follow Logan to California."

Hazel dropped her silverware, creating a loud clatter on the table. Aria just blinked.

"I know it's big news," she continued in an even voice. "He'd asked me to come with him next fall anyway, and just because he's going early doesn't mean I can't go too. My goal is to have the clinic ready in a few months and move out there as soon as I can." She glanced from Hazel to Aria. "I'm going to be counting on you guys to help me while we're gone."

"So you're coming back?" Aria asked.

"Logan's program is only two years. I'm not selling the clinic. Just having someone manage it for me while I'm gone."

"I can do it," Hazel said. "I'll be the office manager. I'll take care of everything." The look of pure excitement on her face helped Layla relax.

Layla giggled. "I knew you'd be the one to volunteer for that." She glanced at Aria, who didn't seem nearly as excited. "What are you thinking?"

Aria took a big bite of her salad. She was particularly good at hiding her emotions, so Layla gave her the time she needed to get her thoughts together.

"So you'll hire another vet, is that it?"

"I was going to ask you if you thought we needed a vet. Burlington has two veterinary clinics, and you could call them for a consult if an extreme case came in." Layla shrugged like she hadn't given this considerable thought. "You could be the vet, Aria."

A look of wonder and panic mingled on Aria's face. "Do you think that would work?"

"We'd need to hire someone to take care of the rescues," Layla said. "And someone to do the special needs therapy, since Logan is leaving."

"I could expand the shelter," Aria said. "Remember how I said I wanted to expand the shelter a few months ago?"

Layla smiled at her friend. "I remember. And yes, you could do that. Hazel would take over the finances." She cut a glance at Hazel, who nodded. "And you would get the profit from the clinic to do what you want. But I am coming back, and I'll want my job at Paws & Claws back when I do. We'll need contracts and stuff."

"I'm sure you've already contacted Matt." Hazel gave her a knowing look. "Right?"

"Maybe." Layla sniffed and picked up her fork. She had indeed already called the lawyer, but Hazel didn't have to be so smug about it. "He'll have the contracts ready in the new year. He's waiting for names and dates and figures from me. I wanted to talk to you two first."

"This is so exciting," Hazel said.

It just felt like a lot of work to Layla, so she simply smiled and went back to her food. *Help everything work out with the clinic,* she prayed again. *And following Logan. When should I tell him?*

Aria seemed to be able to read her thoughts, because she asked, "Have you told Logan you'll be joining him in California?"

"Not yet," Layla said, her stomach turning all the way around. "Let's keep it that way until I figure everything out." She let several seconds go by where she battled her fear before deciding to include her friends in her life.

"What if he doesn't want me back after I move out there?"

"Maybe you should just talk to him," Aria suggested, as if it were that easy.

"I'm still mad at him," Layla admitted.

"What? Why? For moving to start school?"

"No, because he didn't drive the sleigh at my carnival. He said he would, and he didn't."

"You had a sleigh driven by Santa, didn't you?" Aria leaned forward and squinted like she truly didn't understand.

"Yes."

"Then he did what he said he was going to do." She leaned back, problem solved.

Layla didn't argue. She wasn't sure why his abandonment at the carnival had cut her so deeply. Only that it had, and the resulting wound would take some time to heal. And if Layla had one thing at this point, it was time. After all, the contracts wouldn't even be ready for another few weeks.

CHAPTER
TWENTY-ONE

ogan took his laptop into the kitchen and sat at the table with Darren. "What do you think of this one?" He turned the computer toward his brother. "It's furnished."

"That's good." Darren peered at the screen and tapped to advance the pictures. "Looks clean. It's hard to tell online. You can't get a feel for how the place is laid out."

"I can't smell it," Logan said, wondering if he could really get an apartment without seeing it. "Maybe I should just stay in a hotel for a few days."

"You do what you think is right." Darren had been saying that a lot lately. At least he was talking to Logan. He seemed to be the only one. They hadn't talked about Darren being left here by himself, but Logan wasn't going to bring that up. If Darren wanted to talk about it, he would. He hadn't told Logan much of what was bothering him lately, but Logan hadn't prodded him. Darren just needed a few days to sort through things and then he'd lay it all out for Logan.

Meanwhile, Logan had been trying to get everything lined up for a move across the country, buy gifts for his brothers, as well as Bonnie and Rae, Cody and Wade, and Rambo and Honey. He also wanted to get something for Bones and Ginger Ale, as well as the staff at the clinic.

For Layla.

He had no idea what to get for her, but he couldn't leave town without getting her something. It was Christmas, after all.

All he could think to get her was a diamond ring, and he wanted her to pick that out herself. And be speaking to him before he gave it to her.

He sighed and got up to get himself a cup of coffee. "I need to buy a car."

"You should do that here," Darren said. "It'll cost way more in California."

"Yeah, I think I'm going to go up to Burlington this weekend."

"Are you going to get a truck?"

"Probably not. They're more expensive, and Rambo doesn't care about riding in the car, and I feel like I'll stick out less if I'm driving a car and not a truck."

"Yeah, because the cowboy hat won't make you stick out." Darren gave him a wry grin and put his mug in the sink. "All right, I'm headed out. See you in a while."

"Yeah, see ya." Logan stared out the window at all the snow on the ground. Rambo and Honey had trampled most of it in the backyard, creating a mess that thawed during the day and re-froze overnight.

Half an hour later, he arrived downtown, ready to shop until he had everything he needed. Well, that wasn't quite true, but he pretended like it was. He found a pocketknife at the sporting goods store for Darren. The man was seriously addicted to such things, and this one had a flashlight built right in. His brother would love it.

He didn't know Cody or Wade that well, but they were cowboys, and they'd come from a ranch in California. So he figured some winter gear would be nice. He bought them both a pair of fur-lined leather gloves—the same pair Sam had bought for him their first winter in Vermont.

Logan couldn't believe this would be his third winter here, and he lost himself to dreams of sunny California for a few minutes as he wandered the aisles in search of his next find.

When he finally pulled himself back to the task at hand, he looked up to the sight of fishing poles. No one he knew was much into fishing, so he tried the next aisle. He didn't know Bonnie super well, but he did know that Ben lived with Rae and a plethora of pets. Maybe they'd like something animal related. And since Logan wanted to get something for all the dogs in his life too, he paid for his purchases and stepped into the cold in favor of the pet store.

He waited at the light to cross the street, his collar flipped all the way up. With only eleven days until Christmas, quite a few shoppers braved the weather to get their gifts purchased. Logan usually liked going to the pet store, but today it smelled more like urine and soiled straw than normal.

He bought a knobbly ball for Rambo, and a ball made out of braided twine for Honey, who really liked to chew, as he'd learned when he'd found a pair of his cowboy boots looking more like a chew toy than footwear.

He found a new collar and leash for Bones, as he'd bought him the turquoise items the Lab wore this year. But this new deep red would contrast with his white fur well, and Logan smiled as he thought about the dog. He sure would miss Bones.

And Ginger Ale had made so much progress this year. Logan wondered who Layla would get to take the dogs to their therapy appointments and he almost pulled out his phone to ask her. "None of your business," he muttered and left his phone right where it was—in his back pocket.

He bought an assortment of cat and dog toys for Ben and Rae's animals, as well as a set of holiday-themed bandanas for Ginger Ale. *Layla will like those,* Logan thought as he put them in his cart.

It seemed like even the simplest of things brought her to the forefront of his mind. He wondered how long that would take to stop. He didn't want it to stop. He also didn't want to buy her something for Christmas from the pet store.

So he paid for his toys and left, planning to take everything back to his truck. He still had gifts to buy for Sam and Bonnie, Tucker and Missy, and Layla, but he also had a job to do at Steeple Ridge, at least for a few more weeks.

He bumped out of the pet store and into the bright

sunlight, which didn't really provide any warmth at this time of year. It took several moments for his eyes to adjust, and when they did, he caught sight of a curvy blonde who reminded him of Layla.

"Layla," her name left his mouth before he could call it back.

The woman turned.

It was Layla.

Logan's throat turned to sand, and his tongue didn't seem to fit inside his mouth. She said something to the man she was walking with and he continued on his way. Layla took a few steps toward Logan, but it seemed like she was walking in slow motion.

"Good morning, Logan."

The sound of her voice made Logan close his eyes in bliss. What had he been thinking? Breaking up with her? He was *in love* with her. How could he have possibly thought breaking up was the right thing to do? Why hadn't he been more mature? Had a different conversation?

He shook his head to dislodge the swirling thoughts and opened his eyes. "Morning, Layla." He stood there, drinking her in. Noticing the way the sunlight glinted off her snow-colored hair. Breathing in the phantom scent of her perfume, because she stood just slightly out of his reach and he couldn't really smell it. But apparently, he hadn't forgotten it.

"Did you need something?"

Maybe you, he thought. "No," he said stupidly. Most of what he'd done over the past couple of weeks had been stupid. Maybe he could apologize, and beg her to forgive him, and they could be together again.

At least until he left.

She looked tense before glancing over her shoulder. Logan followed her gaze and found the man she'd been with waiting for her down the block.

Instant jealousy painted his entire body, inside and out. "Who's that?"

"My neighbor, Danny Chipman."

"He's married, right?"

Layla tilted her head and stared at Logan. "I don't see how that's a concern for you, but yes. He asked me to help him find something for his wife, Meredith, for Christmas."

"It's a concern for me," Logan said.

"Oh yeah?" Layla cocked her hip, her eyes practically shooting sparks in his direction. "How so?"

"Because you're my—" Logan choked off the last words before they could be spoken.

"I'm not your anything," Layla said. She turned and shaded her eyes. "You made that really clear by abandoning me at the winter carnival."

"I didn't abandon you."

"You sent Darren. Same thing." She strode away. "Have a great Christmas, Logan." She spoke the words, but there was no holiday spirit behind them. No kindness either.

Logan watched her go, realizing how much he'd hurt her, and not just with the break-up either. "I drove the sleigh," he whispered, nowhere near loud enough for her to hear. "I was there, Layla. I didn't send Darren."

Why he couldn't say the words so she could hear them,

he wasn't sure. Just that he needed to wait until the right time. The time when she'd be willing to hear them. When she had time to forgive him. When he could have her in his life again.

Please don't let that take another two years, he prayed as he made his way back to his truck.

That's up to you. The thought came into his mind, but he wasn't sure he'd originated it. He gripped the steering wheel so hard on the way back to Steeple Ridge, his fingers ached by the time he arrived.

"Give me the first step," he said while sitting in the still-idling truck. "Just one step, Lord, and I'll take it and figure things out."

No thoughts entered his mind—his or those from a higher power. He stashed his gifts in his bedroom and headed out to the barns.

He glanced toward the arena where the winter carnival had taken place. He'd been excited to have Layla at Steeple Ridge. Every time she came out to the farm, he enjoyed having her there.

And he knew.

The first step was to get Layla back out to Steeple Ridge.

CHAPTER
TWENTY-TWO

Confusion followed Layla for the rest of the day after meeting Logan on the sidewalk. He'd looked good. Smelled good. She'd wanted to blurt that she'd made some plans to get out to California, but something had held her back. She wasn't sure what.

She liked that he was jealous. Liked that he still thought of her as his. His near-slip at calling her his girlfriend also angered her. Thus, the confusion. Her oscillating emotions only testified to her that she hadn't forgiven him.

Why can't I forgive him?

She pushed open the door and entered the exam room. "Hey, Cocoa Puff." The small Jack Russell terrier growled and then yapped at her, straining against his leash. "How's he doing today?"

Thankfully, Layla's personal life hadn't affected her work at the clinic. She made it through her appointments for the day and sat at her desk. The after-hours silence allowed her time to contemplate, and she twisted to look out the window.

"I'm gonna miss this place," she murmured to herself. It felt strange to be leaving Island Park. When she'd decided to stay five years ago, she thought she'd never leave. She'd also never planned to fall in love.

It also felt strange to not have a planner in front of her. But she'd been trying something different with her idea to turn Paws & Claws over to her friends and get her life packed up and moved across the country.

"The realtor." She shot to her feet when she realized she was supposed to meet Kristen at the apartment—ten minutes ago. She swiped her phone off her desk and dialed as she tried to put on her coat one-handed.

When Kristen answered, Layla said, "I'm on my way," by way of greeting. She didn't want to list the apartment until she spoke to Logan, but she didn't know when that would be. If she had repairs to do, or staging to accomplish, she also needed time to do that. She usually closed the clinic for several days over Christmas and New Year's, and she hoped to get a lot of personal business taken care of at that time.

Secure in her decision, she headed home to find out what she needed to do to close up her life here. The thought of starting a new life gave her a certain measure of hope that carved a smile onto her lips that hadn't been there since Logan had ended things between them.

She listened to Kristin, took notes, and then shut down her mind by doing some online shopping. She could have her family's presents delivered right to them in Boston—

gift wrapped even. Everything else for her dogs, her staff, her friends, she had sent to her. They'd arrive in plenty of time for Layla to wrap and deliver them.

She had everyone crossed off her list by the end of the night. Everyone except for Logan. She'd found the perfect belt for him weeks ago. It still sat in her online cart. Indecision and that persistent confusion needled her, and she left it in her cart and went down the hall to her bedroom without buying it. Maybe tomorrow would have more answers than today had provided.

Layla spent a long time on her knees, expressing gratitude for the things that had worked out. For her friends Hazel and Aria, and their support. For Dr. Gowans in Burlington who had agreed to commute to Island Park and the Paws & Claws clinic every Thursday. He'd also said he'd be on-call if an emergency happened on a non-Thursday and Aria needed him.

She finished her prayer without asking for a single thing, another new tactic she was still perfecting. But she wanted God to know she was grateful for what He did for her, and that she didn't expect more from Him. The blessings He'd given her were already enough, and the love she felt from Him permeated her as she drifted to sleep.

With only four days until Christmas, Layla needed to make a decision about the belt in her shopping cart. If she didn't buy it today, it wouldn't arrive in time to give it to Logan. Today was also the last day the clinic would be open for several days, and Layla had plans to sleep in, relax by trying a couple of new pie recipes, and finish getting her apartment ready to list.

Oh, and she needed to talk to Logan.

She'd been fighting the revelation she'd received weeks ago. She *was* figuring out how to go to California with Logan, but she hadn't told *him* that.

She took a deep breath, clicked to complete the purchase of the belt, and lifted her phone from the kitchen table where she sat. She stared at his name in her contacts, and then typed out a simple text. *I have a gift for you for Christmas. When can we get together?*

She wasn't sure if she'd worded it right. Maybe she should offer to bring it out to Steeple Ridge. Maybe he'd be going to visit Sam for the holidays. Maybe she'd already lost her chance. After all, she'd already had two opportunities to be with Logan.

She forced herself to stop overthinking everything. She hit send. She felt less-Layla-like than ever before as she waited for Logan to respond. Sure, she was still intense, but she hadn't given up.

Like a flash of lightning, she realized that she hadn't given up *because* she was intense. And maybe being intense wasn't so bad in some situations.

Anytime's fine. I have something for you too.

Layla's heart grew two sizes. He had a gift for her too. She pressed her phone to her chest and smiled. She just couldn't believe that things were over between them. She refused to believe it.

How about Christmas Eve? Do you have any family traditions?

Rae invited everyone to dinner. Me and Darren. The other cowboys. Tucker and Missy. The whole crew.

I'll come early then. The clinic is closed that day.

If you could come out here, that would be great, he messaged. I still have to work that day.

Sure, I can come out there. What time?

Bring me a salad for lunch.

Her heart beat at double-speed. Was he flirting with her? She jumped up from the kitchen table and hurried down the hall. She all but beat down Meredith's door and thrust her phone in her friend's face when she finally answered.

"Read this, and tell me what you think."

The seconds it took for Meredith to read the texts seemed like a lifetime to Layla. She finally glanced up, her eyes wide and curious. "Is the salad meaningful?"

Layla giggled, pure giddiness trampling through her. "Yes, he used to bring me salads on Thursdays for lunch. And my girlfriends and I eat at the salad bar at the country club every Monday."

"Then he's flirting with you."

"That's what I thought." Layla took her phone from Meredith. "I ordered his belt."

Meredith leaned into her doorframe. "Good. So you're going to tell him everything, yes?"

Layla's lungs seized, but she said, "Yes."

"So maybe you won't be here on Christmas morning." Meredith gave her a knowing glance.

Layla wrung her fingers. "I'm not sure I've forgiven him yet."

"Well, you have three days to get that done." Meredith pushed off the frame and retreated into her apartment. "You can do it, Lay."

She went back to her apartment, wondering how to speed the forgiveness process. It felt like she'd had plenty of time to work things out, but she simultaneously felt like she hadn't had nearly enough time to process everything and come to peace with it.

Maybe she was being silly. Maybe Logan pawning off the sleigh ride to his brother was no big deal.

No, she thought. *It was a big deal* to me, *and he said he'd do it.* She didn't have to justify how she felt. She just needed to find her way through the forest of her emotions and come out the other side ready to be with Logan again.

Three days.

She had three days to do it.

CHAPTER
TWENTY-THREE

Christmas Eve dawned with the promise of snow. Sure enough, the white stuff started falling by mid-morning, making Logan's already stretched nerves even tighter. He'd been working since Layla's texts to get everything ready for her arrival—and snow was not welcome.

"It's snowing," Darren said when Logan arrived in the barn.

"I'm aware." He brushed the precipitation from his shoulders in exaggerated sweeping motions.

"You ready for this?"

Logan inhaled and tried to center his spirit. "I think so. You think you can convince Layla to get out to the sleigh in the snow?"

"I'll try."

Logan couldn't expect him to do more than that, but his mood only darkened as the minutes until lunchtime passed. He did very few chores, but went out to the sleigh to check that his gift was still there. He rode the path he'd mapped out for the sleigh to make sure it was still sound. He paused in the clearing he'd chosen to stop and really talk with Layla.

In the summertime, the leaves provided a beautiful canopy of shade, but with only branches, they'd get snowed on for sure.

Maybe he should reconsider his plan. But it was his first one, and he'd worked hard on it, and he didn't think he could come up with anything else on such short notice. No, his plan to wear the Santa suit and get behind the reins of his horse and drive the sleigh out to the clearing was all he had. It would have to suffice.

He flipped open the jewelry box to look at the promise ring one more time. He wasn't sure if Layla would like it or not, but it *was* purple, and that *was* her favorite color. The amethyst sat in a sterling silver setting, and the size of it would impress anyone.

He hoped it would impress Layla. He hoped he could express what he needed to, that she would agree to come join him whenever she could, that she'd wear this ring until he could replace it with a diamond.

His stomach lurched and he snapped the lid of the box closed. He couldn't help thinking this was a very bad idea, that no matter what he said, she would stay here and run her clinic, start dating someone else, and be well on her way to building her own life without him by the time he returned.

His phone went off, and he silenced the alarm he'd set.

He glanced toward the farmhouse and could barely make out its edges through the weather. He strode in that direction, being joined by Rambo about halfway there.

"You can't come on the ride," he said. "All right? No dogs allowed." He locked the dog in the mud room and hurried upstairs to change into the Christmas costume.

His phone chimed again and he checked it as he switched out his cowboy hat for the Santa cap.

911. She's here. Tell me you're already in the sleigh.

Not in the sleigh. Logan's thumbs flew across the screen. *Stall her!*

He pulled his cowboy boots back on and sprinted down the steps and toward the back door. He paused and checked to see if she'd parked in the public lot or not. He couldn't see her, but he couldn't hardly see anything through the soupy sky. *Where is she?* he texted to Darren, who didn't respond. He was probably talking to Layla right now.

Logan decided to make a run for it. He felt like the red from head to toe stood out against the grayness and she'd surely be able to spot him from anywhere on the farm.

Thirty yards. Twenty yards. Ten yards.

He arrived at the sleigh and climbed into it. Realizing Layla would be able to see him from afar, he jumped back down. He was supposed to lurk behind his horse, hidden from her sight until Darren delivered her to him.

She didn't come, and Darren didn't text. Logan didn't dare look toward the barns or the farmhouse. Everything around him felt muted, too quiet. Finally, he heard footsteps coming through the snow. Darren saying, "I just want you to see it."

"I can see it," Layla said.

"It has a surprise for you."

Logan groaned silently and rolled his eyes. A surprise? Was that what he was? Should he jump out and shout? He held his ground until the footsteps seemed deafening. Then he stepped around the silver horse, still holding onto the reins.

Layla froze. Darren muttered, "Surprise," met Logan's eyes with hope in his, and left.

"Hey, Layla." Logan extended his hand toward her, a silent plea for her to come to him, link her fingers through his.

She didn't move. Well, she settled her weight on her back foot and folded her arms. She appraised him like he was fruit in the produce section and she was trying to select the highest quality pineapple.

"I'm mad at you," she said, but her lips twitched upward.

"You can tell me all about it on the sleigh ride." Logan went back around the horse, desperate for her to follow him. Relief rushed through him when she did. He helped her into the sleigh and climbed up beside her. He clicked his tongue and Sunshine plodded out into the snow.

"So tell me why you're mad at me." Logan held the reins loosely, hoping she didn't say something he wasn't expecting.

Layla kept her arms clenched around her middle and her voice silent.

"Okay," Logan said. "I'll start. I messed up. I didn't make a plan before I just showed up in your office and said I was leaving in a month. It's totally my fault, but I wasn't sure of anything, and I just acted. No." He threw up one hand. "I *reacted*."

Employing his bravery, he reached over and took her hand in his. "But I made a plan this time, Lay."

"You made a plan?"

"You don't have to sound so surprised."

"But I texted you about exchanging gifts."

"I got you to come out here. And I'm wearing a Santa suit."

She giggled, but sucked the sound back in quickly. "You're driving the sleigh."

"I drove it at the winter carnival too," he said. "That's one of the things. You think I flaked on you, sent Darren to do it. You're wrong. I did it."

She turned fully toward him. "You drove the sleigh at the winter carnival?"

"For two full hours. Same Santa suit."

"I thought you were Darren."

"You didn't even look at me. I feel confident that if you would've looked at me, you would've known."

"I—well, I couldn't look at you. Or Darren." She shook her head. "Whoever it was. You have the same face. I couldn't look at him, because I would've seen you, and everything was too fresh then."

He guided the horse toward the trees, the slip, slip, slip of snow under the runners the only sound. He brought them to a stop. "My second mistake was really my first," he said. "When I found out I could go to California early, I should've talked to you about it. We should've made a decision together. Instead, I made the decision and I cut you out of my life."

He turned toward her. The snow landed coldly on his face, which felt so hot. "I'm so sorry about that, Layla. If I could go back and fix that, I would." He stared out across the landscape, but he couldn't see very far. "So I'm asking you now: Will you come to California just as fast as you can? I don't think I can survive going to college without you."

Logan hadn't allowed his fear over college to surface quite yet. It lingered just below the surface, a constant threat to his mental state.

"You'd be fine," she said.

"I'm better when I'm with you. *You* make me want to be better." All the love he felt for her flowed into him, erasing the panic and the fear. "Which is why I got you this." He pulled the ring box from under the seat and handed it to her.

She stared at it for a full fifteen seconds. Her gaze flew to Logan's. "What is that?"

"Open it and find out."

She shook her head. "I can't. I got you a belt, Logan. A belt." She withdrew a long, slender box from her pocket and tossed it at him. "A freaking belt."

"I need a new belt." He opened the box and admired the brown leather. "I love this. Thanks." He leaned over and kissed her cheek.

"This is a jewelry box." Layla sounded near hysterics.

Logan snatched it from her. "You can't open it until you tell me what you're mad about."

She made a quiet yelping noise. Her eyes searched his, blazing with life and probably anger. Logan couldn't help grinning that she was there. That she hadn't run off.

Everything about her softened. "I think you covered what I was mad about."

"Was?"

"Can I open the box now?"

Logan handed it to her. The lid creaked as she cracked it, and her laughter filled the sky surrounding them.

"It's an amethyst," Logan said. "It's a promise ring. I'm leaving in a week. I'm assuming you won't be able to come then, and I don't want anyone around here getting any ideas that you're available."

She lifted her eyes from the ring to his. He cradled her face in both hands. "I love you, Layla. You're mine, and I'm yours, and that's what the ring represents."

"You're mine," she whispered.

"As long as you'll have me." He closed his eyes and waited for her to kiss him. Her lips felt like a whisper against his, there only long enough to feel for a moment. He moaned, moved his fingers to her hair, and kissed her more forcefully.

"When you're ready," he whispered. "I'll switch that amethyst out for a diamond."

"All right, Santa Claus." She grinned and kissed him again, this time with more passion than she ever had previously.

CHAPTER
TWENTY-FOUR

ayla couldn't believe her gift exchange had turned into her kissing Santa Claus out at Steeple Ridge. She giggled as she pulled away. "Could you take off that ridiculous hat?" She swiped it from Logan's head and sobered. "I like you a lot better in the cowboy hat."

"You and me both," he said with half a growl in his voice.

"I can't believe you bought me a ring." She gazed at the purple gem on her finger. "Did you know I'd already started the process of leaving Island Park?"

He blinked. "What now?"

Layla met his eye. "I decided I was going to come to school with you whether you invited me or not. I think I'll be able to get there in a couple of months." She'd originally thought it would take longer, but with things working out so quickly with Hazel and Aria and Dr. Gowans, her time-line had improved.

"A couple of months?"

"Hazel is going to train to be the office administrator. I'm moving all the financial things I do over to her. So that will take a few weeks." She reached up and ran her hand along the side of his face, a smile forming as a burst of love hit her.

"Aria is going to take over the pet care. If there's an emergency or a procedure she can't do, there's a doctor out of Burlington who's already agreed to help. He'll come to the clinic every Thursday too."

"Wow." Logan blinked at her, the surprise evident in his expression. "You've been busy."

"My apartment goes up for sale just after the new year."

"You're going to sell your apartment?"

"Of course." She nudged him with her shoulder. "You have that big ol' lot all to yourself, and I think you said you wanted to build your life there."

"I do."

"Well, I'm sure we'll get married before you finish school, so I figured I didn't need to keep my apartment here."

"We'll get married before I finish school?"

Layla's confidence faltered for just a moment. Then a teasing twinkle entered Logan's eyes, and she swatted his bicep. "Don't tease me."

"I'd marry you tomorrow, Lay." He touched his lips to hers, and the chilly winter temperatures didn't even bother her.

"Anyway," she said after that bone-melting kiss. She ducked her head. "I'm waiting on the contracts right now. That way, when we come back, I'll be able to go back to the clinic."

"Sounds like you've thought of everything."

She snuggled into his side, thrilled when he lifted his arm around her shoulder. "What about you? How are your plans going for the big move?"

He groaned and shifted in his seat. "I don't want to talk about it."

"Why not?"

He exhaled, his breath hovering before him for a few seconds. "Because I'm not like you, Layla. I don't know where I'm going to live, and I move in a week. I have to go buy a car before I go, and I haven't done that either. Most of my stuff is boxed up. There's that."

"Can't imagine you have a lot of stuff," she said, because she didn't know how to address his frustrated statements about the other stuff.

"I don't, but it's the only thing I've done, so I'd like to claim it."

"I don't think you should be like me," she said quietly.

His arm around her tightened. "I know that."

"I know I can be intense sometimes."

"You can?" He chuckled. "I had no idea. But, Layla, I like it. I like that you make lists and drawings months in advance. It's charming."

"Sure," she said.

"No, really. Maybe you could help me find an apartment. I've been looking online, but I want to be able to walk through them."

"I don't see how I can help then. And hey, another thing you've done. It's not like you haven't even thought about where you're going to live."

"I'm moving on New Year's Eve. Maybe you could come with me. Surely Paws & Claws will be closed for the holiday."

Layla straightened and looked at him. "You want me to come with you?"

"I'm driving across the country, but you could fly back."

Horror threaded through her. "How long does it take to drive across the country?"

"Four days," he said. "Maybe five."

Maybe five days alone in the car with Logan. Eating breakfast, lunch, and dinner with Logan. Holding Logan's hand. Kissing Logan.

"All right, Santa." She leaned over and pressed her lips to his. "It's a deal."

"All right, Layla." He grinned at her. "And we should consider getting married here, before you move to California. Seems silly for you to rent a place there, and for me to rent a place there...." He watched her, and every emotion Layla had ever experienced steamrolled through her.

She loved Logan, but was she ready to marry him?

"You don't have to answer right now," he said, the words rushing over themselves. "But let me know when you might be coming, and—"

"It would be easier on my family—and yours probably

—if we got married here." Layla managed to contain the tremor in her voice. She wasn't sure why the idea of marriage frightened her so much. She had the notebook with the wedding dress sketches, the plans, the checklist.

"I can check and see if we have a spring break at school. That might be a good time." Logan shrugged like he didn't much care, but the desire rode right there in his eyes.

"Let's get a few more details, and then we can decide." Layla sank back into his embrace, grateful for his strength in her life. Grateful for a good many things, only one of which was Logan Buttars.

———

"So you put the bills here." Layla leaned over Hazel, who sat at the computer. She'd just installed the financial software Layla used to keep everything neat and tidy for her accountant. "We have building costs, utilities, and a contingency fund. I put a little in there every month. We have to pay the employees too. That's a bill for the clinic."

She pointed to another tab. "This is where the client bills go. When they're paid, if we have calls out to insurance, and past due notices. You already send those, but I generate the reports for you. I do it once a month, on the fourteenth, and it's as easy as pushing that button right there."

Hazel clicked on the report button, with an icon of a clipboard. "Oh, it is easy."

"Yep. Click 'past due' and the report runs. That's what I give to you, and you send out the reminders."

Layla continued the training and left the clinic exhausted. She hated January. Hated how late the sun rose and how everything seemed perpetually frozen.

When Logan called, Layla startled awake, having fallen asleep on the couch. "Hey, there," she said, not trying to mask the weariness or the frogginess in her voice.

"Did I wake you?"

"Yeah, but it's fine."

"It's only eight-thirty there."

Layla yawned. "Busy day. Plus, there's hardly any sun here. I'm not sure why we want to live here. I checked the weather in California, and it's *much* better than here." She basked in the joy and warmth of his laughter.

"So…." she said. "I booked the church for April fourth."

That silenced him. "Your family is okay with that?"

"The weather isn't usually too bad by then. They can make the drive."

"What did your dad say?"

"You know, he was really great. He said he wanted me to be happy, and you obviously make me happy. So he's fine."

Layla maybe injected a little too much happiness in her voice, because Logan said, "He's probably mad I didn't ask him for his permission to marry you."

"He's not that traditional. And what would you have done if he'd said no?"

"I don't know." Logan sounded haunted, his voice

much too quiet now. Layla knew he still felt inadequate, but she didn't know how to reassure him that he didn't need to be any more than he already was.

She loved that he'd accepted her for exactly who she already was. That he loved her even in her most intense moments.

"I also have an appointment with a dressmaker," she said to lighten the mood. "I think you're really going to like my wedding dress."

"I'm sure I will."

They spoke for a few more minutes, and by the time Layla hung up, she couldn't wait for April to arrive. She sighed, plugged in her phone, and marked off another day on the calendar. She'd only done so twenty-two times, with many more to go before she'd finally have her happy ending.

CHAPTER
TWENTY-FIVE

Logan worked from sunup to sundown, the same way he had at Steeple Ridge. The work for the service dog training program was just a little bit different. He brought Apollo, a loving, attentive German shepherd, with him everywhere he went. Needed to renew his driver's license? Apollo came with. Always only a few inches from Logan's side, he had to sit before Logan could do anything.

He'd been working with Apollo for a couple of months now, and the dog could sit, lay, come, wait, stay, and alert on command now. Verbal and hand only. Logan was extremely proud of his dog—and himself—for how quickly they'd bonded and how well they worked together.

But college was hard. Reading wasn't Logan's favorite thing to do, and studying was something he'd never learned to do. He was starting to figure out his schedule now, but he spent most evenings on his back porch a book balanced on his lap while Apollo got in some play time in the microscopic backyard, the way he was now.

Layla had come with him to find an apartment, and the four-day drive across the country had just proven to him that she was the right woman for him. She was patient when he took wrong turns, persistent when it was time to eat, playful during the long stretches with nothing to do but keep the car on the road.

He'd visited his top three choices for an apartment, and the second one won because of the yard. He'd need one for his service dog, who was now digging in the dirt along the back fence.

"Hey," he said, and Apollo lifted his head, a look of pure innocence on his face. "No. Ball. Get the ball."

The German shepherd abandoned his favorite digging spot and scooped up the orange and blue ball before bringing it to Logan. "Drop."

The dog dropped the ball and lay down. Logan picked up the ball and tossed it, abandoning his studies while he watched Apollo lope after the ball and catch it in his mouth after one bounce.

Another month passed while Logan suffered on his own. He went to class. He worked part-time at a hardware store, where they allowed Apollo to be on the floor with him while he restocked paint cans and power tools and lawn supplies. He called Layla every night.

Finally, spring break arrived. Logan deplaned in New York City to a chilly fifty-seven degrees and rain. He'd left

Rohnert Park, with it's weather at near eighty, and he hadn't thought to bring a jacket.

When he saw Layla, though, everything inside him warmed despite the wind chill and drizzle around him. She jumped from the car and he laughed as he twirled her around, finally setting her on her feet so he could kiss her.

"You can't park here," someone said, and Logan pulled away from the fiancé he hadn't seen in three months.

"Sorry," he said, wrapping one arm around Layla and towing his bag toward her trunk with the other. "Want me to drive?"

"Sure." She climbed in the passenger seat, and he noticed her hair was shorter, her makeup flawless, her clothes perfectly tailored.

He got in the driver's seat and gazed at her. "I love you."

"Mm." She grinned back at him. "Love you too."

"You ready to get married tomorrow?"

"Beyond ready. Though I think I might be more excited about the honeymoon to Hawaii."

"Oh, well, glad to be of service for your trip to Hawaii." He eased into traffic as the attendant on the sidewalk gave him another glare.

She giggled and laced her fingers through his. "It's so cold in Island Park. You'll see."

"Is there still snow on the ground?"

"Tons."

Logan sighed. "Good thing this is an indoor wedding."

"Good thing." Layla leaned over and kissed his cheek, not exactly where he wanted her to. But he waited until they got to her place before kissing her exactly the way he wanted.

The next morning, he stood in front of a full-length mirror with all of his brothers behind him. "This is nice, right?" he asked, tugging on the ends of his jacket's sleeves.

"Real nice." Darren brushed his hand from Logan's shoulder to his elbow, just like the tailor had. "You look great, brother."

He and Darren had been in touch several times a week, and their reunion the previous night had been a lot of hugging and laughing and talking. Logan missed his twin more than he'd thought he would, and he knew he'd left a hole in Darren's life too. At least he was still dating Farrah. He seemed happy and when Logan had asked about her, he always got, "She's great."

"One last thing," Sam said, stepping forward with a hat box. "We all got you a new hat for the wedding." He opened it to reveal a pristine, snow-white cowboy hat. Ben lifted it reverently from the box and handed it to Logan.

Logan wished he could press a button and freeze this moment in time. Him here in a church with all his brothers on his wedding day. A sharp sting penetrated his joy, and it belonged to his parents. They should be here too.

They are, he thought, and he knew in that moment that his parents were indeed with them in spirit.

"Time to get married, bro," Darren said. He'd been taking care of Rambo for the last few months, as Logan wasn't allowed to have any other animals besides those he was training for his program. He'd had to get special permission to have Apollo go with another student for spring break.

"Thanks, bro." Logan grabbed his twin and hugged him. "Thank you, Darren." He embraced the rest of his brothers, and Tucker who stood outside the door like a guard.

"I just saw Layla poke her head out of the bride's room," he said out of the side of his mouth. He lifted his hand to his ear like a real Secret Service agent. "The Barn is moving. I repeat, The Barn is moving."

Logan cocked one eyebrow. "So I'm the barn?"

Tucker shrugged. "Missy and I were tasked with making sure you two didn't see each other before the ceremony."

"What's Layla?"

"The Vet."

"Original," Logan said dryly. "So am I good to go into the chapel?"

Tucker cocked his head, clearly not listening to Logan. Several seconds passed before he said, "Yeah, you're clear."

Darren led Logan into the chapel, which seemed full to capacity. Pastor Gray sat in his usual seat up front, his bright blue eyes sparkling as Logan strode down the aisle with his brothers. They all sat in the very front row, and when Logan turned, he saw Tucker keeping watch in the doorway at the back.

The organ seemed to be playing too softly, and the eyes of everyone in town seemed so heavy. Logan wondered if he should've worn shiny church shoes for his wedding, but as he glanced down the row of men he belonged to, they all wore the same cowboy boots he did. He grinned as the organist paused and switched to the wedding march.

Logan's gaze flew to the doorway, but he didn't see Tucker.

All he could see was Layla. She wore a beautiful white dress that hugged her hips and flared to the ground. The train tailed behind her for yards, and she clung to her father's arm, lifting each foot with precise movement.

The top of the dress had beads and lace, and she'd covered her shoulders with at white fur shawl. It seemed to take an eternity for her to reach him. For her father to pass her over to Logan. With her hand finally secured in his, he turned toward the altar that had been set up.

Pastor Gray stood there and he glanced from Logan to Layla. "Look at you two."

Logan looked at Layla, and she gazed back at him, and his heart swelled with more love than he thought a person could feel. "I love the dress," he whispered.

She giggled and focused back on the preacher.

"Let's get you married, shall we?" Pastor Gray started the ceremony, and all of Logan's nerves and worries disappeared. This time, when he went back to California, Layla would be coming with him. He didn't have to leave her behind. She didn't have to stay because of her clinic. They didn't have to ever be apart again.

"Logan," she hissed.

He pulled himself from his thoughts. "Mm?"

"This is the part where you say 'I do'." Pastor Gray's smile seemed as wide as the Mississippi.

"Oh." Logan met Layla's eyes. "I do."

When she repeated those two words back to him, he barely waited for the preacher to say, "I now pronounce you man and wife," before leaning over and kissing his wife.

———

Read on for a sneak Peet at the next book in the series, **HER PATIENT COWBOY**.

Order it in ebook, paperback, or audiobook by scanning the QR code below.

SNEAK PEEK! HER PATIENT COWBOY CHAPTER ONE

"So you broke up with Farrah?"

Darren bristled at his oldest brother's question. He'd only told his twin, Logan, about the break-up, and he should've planned better for Sam's visit to Island Park.

"She broke up with me," Darren said to the dregs of his cereal bowl. Steps sounded behind them, and he hoped when Sam's wife entered, the conversation would be over.

"She broke up with him," Sam said upon Bonnie's arrival.

Darren sucked in a breath and nearly threw his cornflakes at his brother. "Can we not make it a national event?"

"When did that happen?" Bonnie asked, totally ignoring his question. "I thought you guys were happy."

"Apparently only one of us." Darren slid her a glance

but couldn't truly meet her eyes. He'd been existing in this painful without-Farrah state for sixty-four days now.

Sixty-four days since she'd ended their nine-month relationship. Sixty-four days since he'd spoken to her. He'd seen her at church, of course, which was almost enough to convince him to study the gospel at home.

Most of the time, he made it through his morning chores before he remembered he wouldn't be texting the beautiful blonde through his lunch hour.

Rambo, his brother's dog that got left behind when Logan moved to California seven months ago, whined as if he could sense Darren's discomfort. He would never tell his brother, but he'd been letting Rambo into the farmhouse—and onto his bed—at night. The outdoor Australian shepherd loved having his belly rubbed at bedtime, and Darren liked the companionship.

No, he didn't live alone. But Ben lived in town with Rae now, and Sam had moved all the way to Wyoming with Bonnie, and Logan and Layla had gotten married a few months ago and gone across the country to California.

Darren hadn't gone anywhere. Hadn't done much more than saddle horses, and feed horses, and talk to horses.

Shouldn't have tried to get Farrah to do the same, he thought. If he hadn't pushed so hard about her riding in the Island Park Independence Day parade, maybe she wouldn't have called things off between them.

"...you're coming, right, Darren?"

He looked up at Sam's question, having completely missed the conversation for the past several minutes.

"We're doing what?" he asked, not even trying to hide his lack of attention.

"The cemetery," Sam said, giving him a look as he buttered toast and slid it to Bonnie.

She smiled, but her eyes didn't crinkle around the edges, didn't hold the same level of happiness as usual. Darren didn't blame her. She had traveled a thousand miles while six months pregnant. Afraid to fly, she'd insisted Sam drive them in his pickup truck, and the trip had taken three days.

And they'd come to visit her son's grave. So all in all, the trip couldn't exactly be called a vacation.

"Yeah," Darren said. "I'm coming to the cemetery."

The other two cowboys who'd replaced Logan and Sam came thundering upstairs. Cody and Wade were also brothers, also unmarried, and also not in a relationship. Darren didn't need to feel so isolated, but as the last of the Buttars brothers, he did.

"Morning," Sam said, stepping out of the way so the Caswell brothers could get breakfast.

"Hey," Cody said, grabbing his coffee mug from the dish drainer.

"We're clearing out," Darren said as he stood and danced around his brother to get his dishes into the sink. He followed Bonnie and Sam out to the truck though the cemetery was only about a mile from the farm.

The hay fields that sat between the farm and the cemetery weren't easy to navigate, so Sam went out to the main road and turned north, going back toward town. They drove in silence, and Darren kept his eyes out his window trying to find something about the landscape in Vermont to dislike. He couldn't.

He loved it here; didn't want to leave the way Sam had. Didn't want to start a different career the way Logan had. He loved being a horseman, though the pull of owning his own farm or ranch or boarding stable was appealing. He had enough money from his inheritance to get a decent start, but he didn't want to leave Vermont or Island Park.

So he hadn't even looked—at least until Farrah broke up with him. Then he had seriously considered relocating to a farm of his own. Nothing had caught his eye yet.

Sam parked near Jeffrey's grave, and they all piled out of the truck. Darren hung back, giving Sam and Bonnie their private moment. Bonnie really, who had been married previously, had a child, and then had to bury him after a terrible accident.

Sam kept his arm around Bonnie's shoulders almost protectively, and Darren's heart squeezed at their intimate contact, the easy way they loved each other. Sure, he knew it hadn't always been easy, but everything about them seemed so perfect.

Jealousy lodged in his throat, making it nearly impossible for him to breathe. His lungs kept operating somehow, and he stepped next to Sam and looked down at the grave.

Jeffrey Jones Sherman.

Bonnie bent and ran her fingers along the top of the stone, a sense of sadness in her very movement. Darren took a long drag of air and found a sense of peace in this cemetery he hadn't expected to feel.

He glanced up at the perfectly blue sky, with the wonderfully puffy clouds. The breeze blew across his face, flirted with the brim of his cowboy hat, and he was really glad he was here, in this moment, with his family.

He wasn't sure how much time passed before he became aware of Sam elbowing him.

"What?" he asked in a voice near a hiss.

Sam jerked his head to the right, and Darren's gaze went that way. Another woman had come to the cemetery that morning, and his heart and lungs and every other internal organ seized.

"Farrah," he whispered. What was she doing here? They'd dated for nine months, and never once had she said anything about anyone dying. Island Park was a bustling town, but he would've heard of a funeral—especially if she was affected.

"Go on," Sam said under his breath. "We'll be a while anyway."

Darren looked at his brother. Found hope in his dark eyes that seemed to be swelling within him too. Sam's lips twitched upward. "Be nice to her."

"*She* broke up with me," Darren reminded him as he stepped around his brother and walked away.

Farrah Irvine had intoxicated him from the moment he'd met her. So what if Logan had set up the meeting? So what that it had been in the lobby of the church? Darren hadn't been able to think straight since last fall, and he actually enjoyed the skiwampus ways his thoughts went when he was with Farrah.

He approached her slowly, his hands way down deep

in his pockets. He didn't want to scare her off. Didn't want to intrude. Didn't want to let her get away.

Her dark caramel-colored hair made his stomach ache. He could feel the ghost of it between his fingers as he kissed her, and the temperature suddenly skyrocketed. With his pulse drumming in his ears, and his breath clogged somewhere in his throat, he stepped next to her.

Said nothing.

Held very still.

She finally turned her head to look at him, but he kept his gaze on the headstone at her feet.

Gary Karl Lewis.

Darren had no idea who that was, but he'd passed away three years ago, just before the brothers had come to Island Park.

"How's Bolt?" Darren asked, his voice barely adding its tone to the symphony of wind. He didn't particularly like her cat, but Farrah adored the gray tabby. Today, though, she stood as straight and still as a statue.

The birthdate on the grave marker was today. So Gary had been born today, July seventeenth, sixty-four years ago. Crazy ideas about how it was sixty-four years ago today that he'd been born, and sixty-four days ago that Farrah had broken up with him started circling Darren's mind.

He'd never been one to believe in fate or signs, but everything in him wanted this reunion to be meant to be. Orchestrated by God. Something other than a chance encounter.

Farrah turned back to the marker without saying

anything about her cat. Darren stood two feet from her, but he felt like an ocean separated them.

"Who is he?" he tried next.

"No one," Farrah said.

Yeah, right. Darren didn't believe her though she spoke in her usual calm way. In all the time he'd known her, he'd never seen her so subdued. She didn't exactly call attention to herself, but she usually wore a quick smile, and engaged in lively conversation, and had quirky uses for candy Darren wanted to explore until he knew them all.

He knew she liked to drink soda with a red licorice straw. He knew she liked to separate her fruit candy by color, mixing the reds and oranges, the greens and yellows, and eating the purples all by themselves. He knew she ate chocolate every day, even if it was just a single square from her stash in her pantry.

"I can probably find out," Darren said.

That finally got a reaction from her. She stepped in front of him, blocking his view of the headstone. He looked right into her eyes, and dang if he wasn't excited to be so close to her after being so far apart for so long.

"Don't do that," she said, an edge in her eye that matched the hard tone of her voice.

"I just want—" He cut off so he wouldn't allow the desperation he felt to color his words. "It's a small town," he finally said. "I'll find out anyway."

She cast another look at the stone and then focused on him again. "Don't," she said again. "If I find out you've searched this out, I'll never speak to you again."

He had no doubt she meant what she said. Farrah

always had. The horseback riding in the parade she said she'd never do proved it. So what if he'd found an old picture of her as Island Park's rodeo queen? Leading the princesses on their horses, that glittery tiara on her head? She said she wouldn't do it—and she hadn't.

Hot, electrical pulses shot through his body when she touched his fingers, then his arm. "Please don't make me do that." Her voice wafted across the inches between them, and he was still trying to figure out what she meant and how to get his muscles to stop twitching from her electrifying touch when she stepped past him and strode away.

After several moments, he got his body back in order long enough to turn around. Farrah had already ate up the distance to her car, and she slid behind the wheel of her sleek, black sedan and put on a pair of oversized sunglasses that only made her more exotic, more like a celebrity.

He couldn't tell if she was looking at him or not, but he lifted his hand in a half-hearted wave, wondering if she'd just said she *wanted* to talk to him again.

———

Her Patient Cowboy **is available now!** Order it in ebook, paperback, or audiobook by scanning the QR code below.

ABOUT LIZ

Liz Isaacson writes inspirational romance, usually set in Texas, or Wyoming, or anywhere else horses and cowboys exist. She lives in Utah, where she writes full-time, takes her two dogs to the park everyday, and eats a lot of veggies while writing. Find her on her website at feelgoodfictionbooks.com